Time Off
for Good
Behavior

Time Off for Good Behavior

Lani Diane Rich

WARNER BOOKS

NEW YORK   BOSTON

This book is a work of fiction. Names, characters, places, and incidents are the product of the author's imagination or are used fictitiously. Any resemblance to actual events, locales, or persons, living or dead, is coincidental.

Warner Books

Time Warner Book Group
1271 Avenue of the Americas, New York, NY 10020
Visit our Web site at www.twbookmark.com.

Printed in the United States of America

First Printing: October 2004

10 9 8 7 6 5 4 3 2 1

Library of Congress Cataloging-in-Publication Data

Rich, Lani Diane.
   Time off for good behavior / Lani Diane Rich.
      p. cm.
   ISBN 0-446-69306-5
   1. Attorney and client—Fiction. 2. Female friendship—Fiction.
   3. Conduct of life—Fiction. 4. Divorced women—Fiction. 5. Abusive
   men—Fiction. 6. Unemployed—Fiction. 7. Tennessee—Fiction. I. Title.
   PS3618.I333T56 2004
   813'.6—dc22

                                                              2004005248

Book design and text composition by Nancy Singer Olaguera
Cover design by Brigid Pearson

For Adam, without whom none of this would be possible, because there would only be half of me to do it. I love you.

Acknowledgments

Writing is a bit of a fraudulent business. Here I write this little story, then all these people jump into my life and make it something I could never have made it on my own, and I get all the glory. Or the blame, as the case may be. Fingers crossed, it's the former. Anyway, although it's not nearly enough to express the extent of my gratitude, this is the closest I can come to singing the unsung, so here I go:

To my husband, Adam, who didn't so much as blink an eye when I said, "I think I'd like to quit my job and write, you know, novels."

To my daughters, Sarah and Cecilia, who remind me every day about the one thing that really matters—that they have Cheerios. Now.

To Wanda Woodard, who gave me my opening scene when I had absolutely no idea what I was going to write about, and allowed me to slap her name on my seriously flawed heroine without taking it personally.

To Monica Marcott, whose response to my hysterical "I got

a book deal!" phone call was, "Of course you did. Duh." Now, *that's* faith.

To Chris Baty, whose National Novel Writing Month (www.nanowrimo.org) brainchild forced me to stop editing and start writing.

To the Momwriter Wrimos of 2002, especially Cate Diede, Heather Edwards, and Rebecca Rohan, who trudged through the first draft of the book with me and said, "We think you might have something here."

I'd like to supersize my thanks to my agent, Stephanie Kip Rostan, whose insight, humor, and patience were invaluable to me in trying to navigate this whole publishing maze. Not to mention she also happens to be the best agent in the world. Seriously.

I also bow humbly at the feet of my editor, Beth de Guzman, who did for me the best thing anyone can do for any writer: she made my book better. Big love to Beth.

And last, without trying to sound like I'm pandering, because I really mean this, I'd like to thank everyone who reads this book. You may not realize it, but every time you read a book, you're validating every author who ever thought up a story and, despite the overwhelming odds, said, "I'm gonna give this a shot." You've made dreams come true, and that's one of the most important things a human being can do. So go forth and feel good about yourself. You rock.

Time Off
for Good
Behavior

The court date fell on the Friday of what had been a very bad week for me as an account executive at Hastings Channel 8. Any week in which you take people's money and give them airtime is a bad week, but that week had been unusually degrading, seeing as I'd dropped my card off at more than thirty businesses and had, in no particular order, been screamed at, spit on, and called a bloodsucking leech.

On that Friday morning, I put runs in two separate pairs of panty hose, was forced to wake up my landlady so she could get her nephew in 2B to give my crappy Hyundai a jump, and stained my favorite skirt with cheap, 7-Eleven coffee. By the time the bailiff escorted me to the witness stand, I was already in a bad mood and would have been snippy with Mother Teresa. As it was, the defense lawyer representing the sleaze-balls at Hastings Gas & Electric, who were responsible for the explosion three years ago that destroyed Whittle Advertising and nearly killed me, was definitely not Mother Teresa.

Instead, he was a pencil-faced guy, the kind who couldn't smile without sneering just a little. The sort of guy who had a membership at the most exclusive golf club in town but brought a calculator to restaurants so he could figure out a 15 percent tip to the penny. As a matter of fact, I was pretty sure he was the same guy I spotted at the Wal-Mart last year, demanding that the Salvation Army volunteer stop ringing that damn bell and write him up a receipt.

"How are you feeling today, Ms. Lane?" he asked, looking up at me from the files on the defense table.

"Never better," I lied. The fluorescent lighting was giving me a headache, and I had cramps. But damned if I was gonna let Pencil Face know that.

"Okay, then," he said, approaching me at the witness stand. "Let's get started. What time did the explosion occur?"

"About nine in the morning." I shifted in my seat and rolled my head to loosen my neck. The courtroom was eerily reminiscent of a motel convention room, and it smelled like the plastic covering you put down to protect the floor when you paint. The jury sat on orange plastic seats, most of which wobbled when they shifted their weight. I was sitting on a swivel office chair that squeaked if I turned to the left. I guessed comfortable courtrooms weren't a huge priority when the Hastings, Tennessee, powers-that-be made out the city budget. Either that or someone was buying on the cheap and lining their pockets with the difference. Knowing lawyers and politicians, I'd bet dollars to doughnuts it was option number two.

"And where were you immediately prior to the explosion?"

"Sitting at my desk."

Pencil Face nodded, pacing in front of the witness stand in a piss-poor Gregory-Peck-as-Atticus-Finch affectation. I looked behind him and saw the HG&E reps leaning back with smug expressions and smoothing their five-hundred-dollar ties like they were out for drinks instead of in civil court for blowing up the building in which Whittle Advertising held a corner office. They were the same weasels who came at me in the hospital when I was still hopped up on Demerol and got me to sign papers promising I wouldn't sue if they paid my medical bills.

Fine by me, guys. I never said I wouldn't testify.

I glanced over at Faye Whittle and her lawyer, who were sitting at the plaintiff's table with their arms crossed over their chests. Faye's brown hair hovered like a bird's nest over her thin, puckered face, and all appearances indicated that the tremendous pole she'd had shoved up her ass when I was working for her was still firmly in place. Her attorney was short, fat, and bald and looked alarmingly like a bullfrog.

I turned my attention back to Pencil Face, who continued to toss out the questions. *Did you notice anything unusual?* Yes, I smelled gas. *And what did you do?* I told Faye that I smelled gas. *And what happened next?* Faye told me to stay at my desk and keep working, and she went across the street to call HG&E. *There weren't any phones in the building?* No, it was a new building. That's why the gas line was still being installed. *What happened then?* I needed some sticky notes, so I went into the supply closet and turned on the light. When my hand touched the metal plate on the switch, there was a shock of static electricity. And then . . .

Boom.

"Boom?" Pencil Face looked up from the notes he was flipping through at the defense table. My irritation surged.

"Yeah," I said. "Boom. The place went up. So did my hair, and the sleeves of my dress, which flamed up and burned my hands and my arms, although I didn't notice so much because I was busy trying to figure out why my ass was suddenly wedged between the back wall and the filing cabinet." I stared point-blank at one of the smarmy HG&E reps as I spoke. He never met my eye. Big surprise.

"Ms. Lane, I think that word is inappropriate."

"What word? *Cabinet*? Or *wall*?" I blinked innocence, trying to grate on his nerves and, from what I could tell, succeeding quite nicely.

"I think you know which word." Pencil Face turned his beady, narrowed eyes from me to the jury and went on. "So you smelled the gas."

"Yes, I smelled the gas."

"And yet you didn't leave the building? You chose to stay and work even though you knew you were in danger?"

I shifted in my seat. It squeaked. "Faye told me to stay."

"But you smelled the gas?"

"Yes," I repeated through clenched teeth.

"Well," Pencil Face said with a well-practiced and humorless laugh, "I guess I'm just wondering why, if the smell of the gas was so obvious and strong, you stayed in the building."

I narrowed my eyes to slits. "Exactly what are you getting at?"

"What I'm *getting at*, Ms. Lane," he said, his tone thick with mockery, "is that you didn't really smell gas, now, did you?"

I glanced over at Faye and the Bullfrog, who showed no indication that he was planning on objecting to Pencil Face's blatant badgering. Once again, Faye Whittle was proving useless to me. I looked back at Pencil Face.

"Are you insinuating that I'm lying?"

"Oh, I'm not insinuating anything," he said, wisely backing away from the witness stand and turning to the jury. "I'm just saying it begs the question."

"Excuse me?" I stood up. The judge let out a heavy sigh. I ignored it. "Look, you little shit—"

"Ms. Lane." The judge's tone was sharp, but I didn't care. This was personal now.

"Yes, I smelled the gas. But it could have been anything. It could have been next door. I could have slopped some gas on my shoes when I filled my tank that morning. I turned on a light, for Christ's sake. It's not like I smelled gas and lit up a goddamn cigarette, you pencil-faced butt munch."

"Ms. Lane!" I heard the judge slam down her gavel, but I kept my glare locked on Pencil Face. This was one of many moments in my life when it would have behooved me to remember the words my father repeated to me often while I was growing up: *Wanda, sometimes a battle is worth fighting. And sometimes you just have to know when to shut the hell up.*

I leaned forward on the railing that enclosed the witness stand. "And another thing, jackass . . ."

"Ms. Lane!" The judge was pounding her gavel.

". . . if I for one minute thought that staying in that office was going to get me a front-row ticket to six weeks of painkillers and bathing in Neosporin, you would have had to nail-gun my ass to the floor to keep me in that place."

". . . held in contempt of court if you don't sit down . . ."

"You wanna talk about poor judgment? Let's talk about the fucking dipshits who left an open gas line piping into the building."

Pencil Face looked at me, his beady little weasel eyes glittering in the face of conflict. My chest was heaving with the force of my ragged breath. He moved in close and gave me an empty smirk.

"Thank you for saving me the time of bringing someone in here to testify about your character," he said, his eyes drifting down to my breasts and back up to my face, reminding me that I was a woman and he'd use that against me if I pushed him.

I almost heard it, the pop and hiss as my fury erupted. I pulled my arm back and swung at Pencil Face. He'd turned to glance at his sleazy HG&E guys, so he didn't see me coming. It was luck, and not reflexes, that made him move a smidgen to the left. There was a crack, and I felt the cheap witness stand railing give out underneath me. Pencil Face gave a girly screech and jumped out of my way as I fell forward. I can still hear the sound of my head as it slammed with a sickening clunk on the thin carpet that covered the floor, and I can still hear my father's voice seeping up from my memory, laced with disappointment: *Sometimes you just have to know when to shut the hell up.*

It took me a while to recognize the hospital room for what it was when I woke up. At first, everything was a pale blur, and as my vision returned, the pieces came at me individually. The tall swivel tray sitting by my bed. The IV pole at my side. The framed poster of a generic landscape. The window with venetian blinds hanging halfway down. I took it all in, unalarmed, too groggy to put the pieces together and panic properly.

A rhythmic squeaking noise grew louder and paused, and then the door opened. A nurse in pink scrubs entered, carrying an IV bag filled with clear fluid. She hummed the theme to *Green Acres* as she puttered around the room, and didn't notice I was awake and watching her until she finished switching the bags on the IV pole.

"Oh, Miss Lane!" she said brightly, her southern accent dripping with honey. "It's good to have you back."

She had the largest smile I'd ever seen. It took over her entire face, her eyes barely showing under the pressure from her massive cheeks. I opened my mouth to say something, but only a harsh whispered "Unnnnhhh" came out through the sandpaper in my throat.

"Oh, honey," she said, putting her warm hand on my arm. "Don't try to talk yet. Give yourself a minute to adjust."

She reached over and pulled the blankets up farther on my torso, making me feel like a preschooler at nap time.

She smiled again. "Miss Lane . . . May I call you Wanda?"

I gave her a small nod, which I immediately regretted as a sharp pain hatcheted its way through my skull. The panic began to form then, dull and throbbing in my gut. The nurse must have caught it in my expression because her smile waned enough for me to see the concern in her eyes, and she gave my arm a comforting squeeze.

"Now, Wanda, I know it's kinda scary waking up in a hospital, but you're gonna be just fine, and my mama didn't raise no liars, so don't you worry." She bit her lip and looked around the empty room. "Is there anyone you'd like me to call for you, honey?"

I blinked and made a slight "no" movement with my head. There was no one.

"Okay." Her smile reappeared, tighter this time. That's how people who have someone tend to react to people who have no one. She tucked a call button remote into my hand. "Well, my name is Vera, and I'm your nurse, so if you ever need anything, you just hit this button and I'll come running, okay?"

I didn't want to risk the sandpaper, but I desperately wanted some water, so I flitted my eyes from the cup and pitcher sitting on the swivel tray back to Vera as she talked, hoping she would take the hint before the movement made my head explode. She followed my eyes to the pitcher.

"Oh, honey, did you want some water?"

I gave her a small, grateful smile. She nibbled on her lip. "Well, darlin', it's been a while since you've had anything in your tummy. I'm gonna go get Dr. Harland—he'll be so glad to hear you're awake—and we'll just see if he says it's okay, all right?"

With that, Vera and her tremendous smile squeak-squeak-squeaked out of the room. I blinked twice and looked around again, trying to gain control of my focus, but it wasn't worth the pain of keeping my eyes open, so I closed them and leaned back into my pillow. My arms and legs felt like deadweights, and while I could move them, anything exceeding a slight shift was more trouble than it was worth. There was a familiar tune playing, probably coming from the radio at the nurses' station, and I tried to concentrate on it, but it faded away before I could place it. I thought about the cup and pitcher on the tray next to my bed, but unless I developed some telekinetic ability in the next few minutes, I'd have to wait for Vera and the good doctor.

The door opened, and a short man in a white coat came in, with Vera squeak-squeaking behind him. The doctor smiled, sat on the side of my bed, and put his hand on my arm. It was warm. "Hi, Wanda. I'm Dr. Harland."

Vera stood behind Dr. Harland and didn't catch my meaningful glances toward the water pitcher this time. I gave up and listened to the doctor.

"We're glad to see you awake," he said. He was a tiny man with dark skin and deep-set eyes. He couldn't have been more than forty, but smile lines radiated from his eyes and curved around the edges of his mouth like cheerful parentheses. I can handle cranky people, and I can handle antisocial people, but smiley people always put me on edge. In my experience, they tend to be irritating or crazy. Often both.

Dr. Harland explained my condition to me. Apparently, the cheap Berber carpeting in the courtroom was laid directly on top of a cement floor, with no padding. Shocker. The sickening clunk had been the sound of my skull fracturing, and I had ended up with a concussion and some swelling of the brain. I had been in a light coma for five days. I would be on painkillers for a week or so and would probably experience some headaches, but overall I was a very lucky woman. I found the strength to nod, showing him I understood, but my mind stuck on the word *lucky*. Just went to show what he knew.

Dr. Harland squeezed my arm. "I'm gonna go, let you get a little rest, but I'll be back in to check on you in a little while, and then we'll start on that recovery, okay?"

I gave another brief nod. Pain radiated through my head. He flashed me one cheerful smile and left. I closed my eyes and rested my head on the pillow. The room started to spin. I opened my eyes again, and Vera was standing by my bed, sticking a bendy straw in the water. "Dr. Harland told me we could try some water. You ready, honey?"

I parted my lips and drank. The first few sips went well, but I soon learned that it's a bad idea to introduce anything quickly to a stomach that has been empty for five days, and I started to gag. Vera reached for the bedpan with practiced ease, and I proceeded to make a sterling first impression.

"Aw, honey," she said when I was done. "Don't you worry. We'll just give that a try again later, okay?"

I tried to give another tiny nod but found just enough strength to rest my head back on the pillow. As it turned out, skull fractures hurt like a mother.

"You get a little more sleep, honey, and I'll be back to check in on you in just a little bit." She reached up and checked my

IV, then gave my arm another gentle squeeze and winked at me, her eyes succumbing to another tremendous grin. "And don't you worry about a thing."

She squeak-squeaked through the door, and I was alone. I sank back into the pillow and stared at the ceiling. The familiar tune wafted back into the room, and I fell asleep trying to place it.

᎒Ꭹ

"I'm fine, George. Really. Fine." I held the phone away from my ear and leaned back on the pillows, thanking God for each and every one of the five thousand miles between Tennessee and Alaska.

"I'm gonna take off work. Come down and see you." George's voice was competing with pay phone static and the sounds of oil workers passing through the hallways of the compound where they lived while they were on the slope. "I'll get a job down there. I'll take care of you. We can start a family, get a small house with a fireplace. Just like you always wanted. Come on, baby."

"We're divorced, George. Don't call me baby." I put my hand to my forehead. My headache was raging.

"But I love you," he said. His voice was quiet. My stomach was turning. I looked at the phone cradle as the chorus in my head sang, *Hang up, hang up, hang up.*

"Look, George, I'm fine. I'm getting out of the hospital soon, and I'm going back to work. I really don't have time for a visit."

Silence. Silence was never a good sign with George. It could mean anything. He could be crumpling under the emotional strain. He could be plotting to kill me. Anything was possible.

"Stay in Alaska," I said finally. "Please. I'm fine."

The door to my room opened. A tall guy in a suit gave me a tentative smile from the doorway. He had lawyer written all over him, but I was willing to give him the benefit of the doubt. Maybe he was from the local Bible college, visiting the hospitalized friendless, doing his Good Samaritan deed du jour.

"George, I have to go. Don't come down here. I'm sorry they even called you." The last time I'd been in Hastings General, George and I were still married, and I'd put his information down on the "in case of emergency contact" sheet. A decision, like so many others, that was coming back to haunt me.

"Baby, I love you. I've been going crazy up here, not knowing if you were okay. I need to see you."

I sighed. My stomach knotted up. Time to pull out the big guns. "George, the restraining order is still in effect. If you show up here, you'll go to jail." I looked up and gave a "What are you gonna do?" eye roll to the guy, whose tentative smile went swiftly south.

There was a frustrated huff, something that sounded like *bitch*, and then the line went dead. *He won't come,* I told myself. The last thing George wanted was another run-in with the Tennessee cops, who didn't have much patience for outsiders with attitude problems. He was still wanted on a DUI and an unregistered-weapons charge; the restraining order merely sealed the deal that would keep him out of the state. I put the phone down and pressed my fingertips against my temples.

"Maybe I should come back later," the guy said.

I waved my hand dismissively. "If you're gonna come back, you might as well stay."

He nodded and stepped toward me, a crooked smile snaking up one side of his face as he held out his hand. "Hi, Wanda. My name is Walter Briggs."

I smiled back as I took his hand. He had brown hair and wire-frame glasses, and his handshake was firm, but not like he was trying to prove anything. He was that Jimmy Stewart kind of handsome, the kind you didn't notice much until he unleashed that crooked smile on you and then *hoo-wah*.

"I'm a lawyer," he said.

Hoo-whatever. I withdrew my hand and crossed my arms, narrowing my eyes at him.

"I knew it."

"I'm sorry?"

"Bible college, my ass," I muttered.

"Excuse me?"

I crossed my arms and went on attack. "Couldn't even wait until the painkillers wore off, could you?"

His eyebrows knit slightly, and his head tilted a bit. Nice whack at innocence, but I wasn't buying it. He looked at me in silence, and I widened my eyes, speaking slowly so he'd understand.

"I'm not signing anything."

"Okaaaaaay," he said.

"So you can just run along back to Pencil Face and tell him I'm not falling for that trick."

The crooked smile snaked up a notch in a manner that was not at all attractive. *Not one bit.*

"Pencil Face?"

"Your boss, the defense lawyer for those HG&E guys."

His eyebrows raised in understanding. "Oh. You mean John Douglass."

I rolled my eyes and flicked my hand at him. "Run along. I'm not signing anything. You're wasting your time."

He gave a low chuckle that was also not at all appealing. "Why don't you let me worry about my time?"

"I was trying to be polite," I said through clenched teeth. "I care about *my* time."

He nodded, reaching into his pocket and withdrawing a business card. "Then I won't take up much more of it. Like I said, my name is Walter Briggs. Although I am familiar with John Douglass—sorry, Pencil Face—I'm not associated with him."

I looked down at the card. It was plain with black type: "Walter Briggs, Attorney-at-Law." I looked back up at Walter, who was smiling down at me.

Okay. Maybe the smile was a *little* attractive.

"So if you're not associated with Pencil Face, what are you doing here?"

His eyes tightened a bit, but his mouth didn't skip a beat. "I heard about what happened at the courthouse. Based on my research, you have a decent case against the city. I thought I'd come by and offer to help you, if you decide to pursue legal action."

I ran my eyes over the card again and then up to his face. "You don't look like an ambulance chaser."

His amused expression waned a bit. "I'm not."

"Then why are you here soliciting for business?"

"Are you this hard on everyone you meet?"

"Not everyone," I said, feeling a smile play on my lips despite my better judgment. You'd have to be blind and deaf to not smile at Jimmy Stewart. "Just the lawyers."

Vera entered, carrying my dinner tray. Judging by the smell, I'd finally made it to the A-list of hospital inmates allowed to eat something other than Jell-O and beef bouillon. Walter stepped back to give her room.

"I'll let you enjoy your dinner," he said, his hand reaching for the door. He started to go, then turned his head and shot another grin at me. "I'm glad you're feeling better, Wanda." He looked over at Vera and flashed her a bigger grin. I was not at all jealous.

"Have a nice day."

And then he was gone.

Vera raised her eyebrows at me. "Cute."

"I guess," I said. "So, I'm getting real food now?"

"You guess?" she said. "Honey, you gotta appreciate a boyfriend looks like that. I wouldn't kick him outta my bed for eating crackers, I'll tell you that much."

"Boyfriend?" I said. "I just met him."

She gave me a quizzical look. "But he was here every day when you were in the coma. I was wondering where he went . . ."

"Here where? In the hospital?"

She shook her head. "Here *here*, in your room."

"Every day?" I said, trying to picture Jimmy Stewart as a psycho stalker. Couldn't do it. "All day?"

"No," she said, "not all day, but he's been coming by, stopping in your room, checking on you. Sometimes he'd sit for a spell. We all just assumed he was your boyfriend. I was surprised when you said not to call anyone for you; if that man was in my room every day, I'd have him on speed dial."

"Well, sorry to be the sugar in your gas tank, but . . ." I handed her his card. She read it, rolled her eyes, and handed it back.

"Lawyers," she said, shaking her head in severe disappointment.

"Preaching to the choir, sister," I said.

She crossed her arms, stared for a moment at the doorway where he'd just been, and shrugged. "Still wouldn't kick him out of bed." She turned and gave me a bright smile. "Well, you eat your dinner, honey, and happy birthday!"

I put my fork down. "Happy birthday?"

She nodded and seemed at a loss for words for a moment. That impression was fleeting. "October twenty-sixth, right? According to your chart?"

"Yeah," I said. *Crap.* "I'm thirty-two today."

She smiled, about to say something chipper, then apparently thought better of it. "Honey, where's your family?"

I picked up my fork. "New York."

She paused a beat, wisely choosing not to pick at that thread. "Are you sure there's no one we should call? I know you informed us not to contact your husband again—"

"Ex-husband." I poked at the chicken on my plate. It resisted. "This thing is dead, right?"

"Wanda?"

"Are these instant potatoes?" I let a clump fall from my fork
with a dull splat. "Five thousand dollars a minute for a hospital
bed, and you guys can't afford real potatoes?"

"I'm about to go on break," she said. "I was wondering if
you'd . . . maybe . . . Would you mind if I ate with you?"

"Don't pity me, Vera," I said, not looking at her. "I'm used
to being alone. I like it that way."

She crossed her arms and jutted one hip out with attitude.
"Well, *I* don't like eating alone, and I thought that sitting in
here with you might be nice, but you're quickly changing my
mind."

I smiled. Vera had teeth. Good for her. "Could you bring
me some real potatoes?" I asked.

She smiled and patted my knee. "I'll see what I can do for
you."

She squeaked on out. My birthday. Goddamn.

I sighed and poked at my chicken, then stopped. The tune.
That same damn tune. Again. I listened carefully. It was faint.
Sort of classical. I could hear a piano approaching some sort of
crescendo. I'd heard it before, I knew I had, but I just couldn't
place it . . .

"Hope this potato is real enough for you," Vera said as she
squeaked back into the room. Damn nurse shoes.

"Shhhh!" I said, holding up my hand. She froze. I lowered
my hand. It was gone.

She moved forward and placed the foil-covered potato on my tray. "You okay, Wanda?"

"Yeah," I said, watching her as she grabbed a tray from the empty bed on the other side of the room. "It's just that song. It's driving me crazy."

She settled on the bed next to me and situated her food. "What song?"

I raised my knife, motioning out the door. "I don't know. Whatever music the nurses keep playing at the station."

Her eyebrows knit. "We're not playing any music."

I took a bite from the dinner roll. I had to admit it wasn't bad. My stomach clamored for the real food, growling for more. "Then whatever you're piping through the PA system."

She shook her head and gave a gentle laugh. "I don't know what you're talking about. We don't play music here. It's impossible to find something everybody likes, and the way people complain . . ."

"Well, there's something," I said. "I keep hearing it."

She sat back and stared at me for a moment. "Should I get the doctor?"

I shook my head, about to speak, but then the music faded in again.

"See?" I said, motioning vaguely into the air. "Ugh. It's driving me nuts. I know I know that tune, but it keeps fading out right when I'm about to place it."

I trailed off as the crescendo approached. Vera watched me carefully. It faded away.

"Dammit. Do you know what that song is?"

Vera stood up. "I'm going to go get the doctor."

"No. Why? Is it his music?"

Vera inhaled. "There's no music."

I rolled my eyes at her. "What do you mean there's no music? It was just right there, you heard it."

Vera shook her head. "There's no music, Wanda."

I put my fork down. My stomach stopped growling. "Of course, there's music."

She shook her head again and stood up. "I'm gonna go get Dr. Harland."

I waved my hand at her. "No. Don't bother him at home."

"He's on today, I'm pretty sure," she said, heading toward the door. "I just saw him about an hour ago."

I swallowed. Nodded. Vera left. I looked out the window, the streetlights blurring as my eyes teared up. Alone on my birthday. And crazy to boot. I could hardly wait for thirty-three.

⊙⊚

I was released from the hospital a week later. The doctors were pleased as punch that I hadn't suffered any major trauma, that I sailed right out of a light coma and into recovery. I still felt a little woozy when I got up fast, but they were sure that another two weeks of rest at home would be the best medicine.

"And what about the music?" I asked Dr. Harland when he was regaling me with praise for my miraculous recovery. We were sitting on my hospital bed, waiting for the damn nurse to come with the damn wheelchair and wheel me out of the damn hospital despite the fact that I could walk out of it on my own.

Damn rules.

Dr. Harland smiled at me. He was a "Go get 'em, sport" kind of guy, and his perpetual cheerfulness—especially considering he was five foot one and should have been good and pissed off—was rather unsettling for me.

"The music?"

"Yes. The phantom music I keep hearing that no one else can hear. Remember?"

"Well, now, Wanda, the thing is . . . we've tested you for tinnitus . . ."

"It's music, not ringing," I said through clenched teeth. I'd been hearing about friggin' tinnitus for the past week. I was sick to death of tinnitus. "I'm telling you, there's music. I hear it. There must be a reason why."

He sighed, looking genuinely concerned. He was so earnest I wanted to smack him. "Wanda, we've checked your ears, and their physical condition is perfectly normal."

I could feel my nails digging into my palms as I clenched my fists. "Well, something's going on. It's not my imagination. I'm not dreaming it; I'm hearing it."

"Hmmm." Dr. Harland pursed his lips. "Maybe we should get you an appointment with Dr. Angibous."

I raised my eyebrows. This sounded hopeful. "Dr. Angibous? Who's Dr. Angibous? Some kind of ear specialist?"

Dr. Harland gently shook his head. "He's a psychiatrist."

"I'm not seeing a shrink," I growled. "It's not in my head. I'm not crazy."

"Of course not," Dr. Harland said. "I'm not saying that. All

I'm saying is, there is no *physical* reason for your condition." He reached over and patted my hand. "You could pursue it with a neurologist, but since the symptoms are slight and don't really affect your functionality, you might save yourself time and money and just get used to it. Eventually, it might just go away on its own."

"Go away on its own? Is that what they teach you in medical school? If you have no fucking idea what's going on, just tell the patient it'll *go away on its own?*"

Dr. Harland shrugged and smiled at me like the most angelic little human being on the planet, and all I wanted to do was shake him and yell, "You're short!" until he got angry and bitter like a normal person.

But then the nurse arrived with my wheelchair, and I stepped in, complaining all the way to the hospital exit that I was perfectly capable of walking down the damn hallway by my damn self.

My apartment was a small, one-bedroom number with an open area for kitchen, dining room, and living room and just enough windows to make the builders free from liability for the clinical depression that tended to overtake the tenants in my building. It was the place I'd escaped to when George and I split, and although I could probably afford a nicer place, I stayed. I'd become a staunch subscriber to the "rainy day" theory of life. I'd had enough rainy days to know that more were always coming.

I spent most of my recovery period reading. I have this thing about books. I think I got it from my mom. She used to read about five a week. When I was young, when my father was just starting his work with his practice in Manhattan, we were dead broke. Dad worked a lot, and the commute into the city ate up a couple of hours each day, so mostly, it was just me and Mom entertaining ourselves. Every Wednesday we'd walk down to the library together and choose our books. She'd recommend her favorites to me, classics like *Alice in Wonderland* and *Charlotte's Web*. I'd usually choose a Judy Blume book just to bug her. She hated that I'd waste my time reading about children whose parents cared so little about them that they'd name them Fudge.

I remember sitting in the living room with her, just the two of us, reading in silence. We each had our own chair flanking the standing lamp in the corner. She would curl up with a cup of tea and read *Anna Karenina*, which she read every summer. She'd cry every time. To this day, I still haven't read that book. I didn't understand why people would want to read books that made them cry.

I was supposed to be recovering at home for two weeks on Dr. Harland's orders, but within five days of my release from the hospital, I was going bat-ass crazy in that apartment. I'd dusted the top of my refrigerator. I'd alphabetized my CD collection. I'd emptied out the bag of pill bottles and random et cetera I'd brought home with me from the hospital and lined them up in my medicine cabinet by size. I even stuck Walter Briggs's business card in the corner of my bathroom mirror, contemplating taking him up on suing the city, partly so I could have someone to talk to and partly because I, like Vera, would probably not kick him out of my bed for eating crackers.

That was the final straw.

On Thursday morning, a good week before I was supposed to return to work, I got up, got dressed, and headed out to surprise my coworkers at Channel 8.

Channel 8 staked out the northern half of a strip mall, while the southern half was occupied by a tanning salon and a florist, neither of which was advertising on our air. To me, that always summed up the character of the station: so pathetic that even our neighbors wouldn't play with us.

I pushed my way through the glass doors into the station. In its previous incarnation, it had been a furniture store, with white walls and gray carpeting that were intended to play bridesmaid to rolltop desks and oak dining sets. When Channel 8 moved in, they immediately put up gray cubicles in the open area to create a "team atmosphere." The only atmosphere it created was that of a bunch of gophers living in a huge, dusty rice cake.

Susie Huffman, possibly the least savvy salesperson on the planet, was sitting at my desk when I arrived, picking through my files with her long acrylic nails. Susie was twenty-two going on twelve. She actually believed potential clients when they promised to call her back once business slowed down. She cried an average of five to seven times a week, although on occasion it worked for her. Tom Shelty, the owner of Hobby Hound Dog, was so freaked out by her crying all over his classic model car display that he'd signed an annual right on the spot.

Susie had been handling my clients for me, and I dreaded finding out how little of my paycheck I'd be seeing for the next month or so. Hell, with Susie handling things, I might even owe the station money.

She looked up to see me and slammed the file drawer shut. "Wanda!" she said with false enthusiasm. She might have

pulled it off if she could have hidden the tremor in her voice.
"You're back early!"

I saw a few gopher heads pop up over the tops of the cubicles, the same way they always did when they sensed the
ground was about to shake. I sidled past Susie and started
rifling through the pile of mail and memos on my desk.

"Yeah. I'm fine now. I'm back." I sat on the edge of my desk
and folded my arms. "All right, Susie. Out with it. How much
of my business did you lose?"

"Well," she started, biting her lip, "Activity Center decided
they didn't want to go on air until school starts again in the fall.
Feeney Contracting said they'd get back to me in first quarter.
And Finnegan's Chevrolet is on Trudy's list now."

"What?" I grabbed the file from her. "Trudy's list? What
the hell is my biggest client doing on Trudy's list?"

Trudy Laverly was the devil in an inappropriate dress, the
kind of person who lied to her clients to get them to sign a contract and then let the sales assistant take the heat when dis-
crepancies were found. I glanced over at her cubicle, which was
conveniently empty. No doubt she'd heard the distinctive roar
of my crappy muffler and went to hide in the bathroom. Trudy
may have been evil incarnate, but she wasn't stupid.

I looked at Susie and tried to tone down my exasperation.
She may not have been the sharpest crayon in the box, but she
wasn't conniving or manipulative, so that put her head and
shoulders above most of the other people there. Of course,
Channel 8 would chew her up and spit her out in six months or
less, but that was really her problem.

"Susie, calm down. If you bite your lip any harder, you're going to need plastic surgery. Don't worry. I'll get Finnegan's back." Everything was the end of the world in television, and it got on my nerves. Some piddly client placing three hundred dollars a month on overnights misses a spot, and people were screaming and yelling and crying and cursing like they just spotted the Four Horsemen shopping at the 7-Eleven on Main.

Susie shook her head. "I don't know, Wanda. Blaine said that Finnegan's needed more personal attention."

"Yes, and I'm a person. I'll handle it. Stop fidgeting. Jesus. Get a prescription, will you?"

"But Blaine said—"

"Don't worry about Blaine. I'll handle Blaine."

Blaine Dowd was the general manager at Channel 8, and he was exactly what you'd expect when you heard the name Blaine: a pale-faced, sweaty-palmed, spineless weasel. He'd been fired from every job he ever had, usually for incompetence, although rumor has it that once or twice he'd been caught taking money from petty cash. Eventually his dad, Edgar, who owned Channel 8 along with half the media outlets in east Tennessee, put Blaine in charge of the station, where he could keep an eye on him. The simulated rice cake was the first of many stupid things Blaine had done with the station. We were number two in the market when he took over; now it was a good Nielsen book when we could show evidence that anyone had watched at all.

I looked over toward Blaine's office, which was a big glass

fishbowl in the southeast corner of the building. He was on the phone. I shooed Susie away from my desk and headed toward Blaine's office, slamming the door behind me as I entered.

"What the fuck, Blaine?" I was loud and could see a few more gophers pop up in my peripheral vision. Blaine had gotten off the phone right quick when he saw me coming. Probably a wise move.

"Wanda, I'm glad you stopped in," he said, motioning toward the chair across from him. He sat down and clasped his hands together. "We need to talk."

"No shit we need to talk." He bristled at the language. The worst word I'd ever heard Blaine say was *drat*, a fact that made it almost impossible for me to conduct a conversation with him without swearing.

"So I guess Susie told you." He smiled one of those quivery-lipped smiles that you get from people who have never had a genuine good feeling in their entire lives.

"Yeah, she told me."

"Well, then, there really isn't much more left to say, is there? There are some empty boxes down in Cate's office. Please have your things cleared out by the end of the day."

My things? I stared at Blaine as my mind processed what he was saying.

His eyes flashed in a panic. "Susie didn't tell you."

"Susie told me that Finnegan's is on Trudy's account list. She didn't tell me that you're firing me. You're *firing* me?" I stood up and leaned over his desk, although you'd think the knock on the head in the courtroom would have cured me of heat-of-the-moment behavior. What can I say? I wasn't a quick learner.

"Look, Wanda, it said clearly in your contract that if you didn't meet your sales quota for three weeks in a row, the station would be within its rights to find a replacement for your position." He grabbed a stress ball and squeezed it, then tried to work up a smile. "You've been gone three weeks."

"I was in a *coma*, Blaine," I said, speaking slowly so he would understand. The office joke was that Blaine had a brain disorder that translated anything anyone ever said to him into "blah-blah, blahbiddy, blah-blah-blah."

I grabbed the stress ball from his hands and stared him in the eye. "You can't fire someone for being in a coma. It's illegal."

His index finger shook as he pointed to a photocopy of my contract, which was conveniently sitting on his desk. "You see, it says right here—"

"I know what it says, Blaine." I sighed. This was pointless. "Where's your dad?"

Blaine was trying to maintain an air of composure, but I could practically see the wet spot forming at his crotch. "I'm the general manager here."

"Oh, please, Blaine. You're the general joke around here." Blaine gasped, and a flush crept up his neck. "I know you've been wanting to can me for a long time, but how stupid are you? I mean, really. I've got like twelve fucking lawsuits here."

"Wanda, you know that language is inappropriate, and actually, if you refer to the employee manual, it is grounds for termination."

"Oh, bite me, you little son of a bitch. Now, where's your dad?"

"On a cruise, and he won't be back until next Friday." He cleared his throat, stood up, and smoothed his tie. "But that doesn't matter because the decision is mine, and there isn't much left to say on the matter." His palm left a sweat mark on his tie. He looked like he was about to throw up.

I took a moment. It wasn't so much that I minded losing the job. Selling television advertising was a degrading existence, and God knows working for Blaine only made that reality more biting. I'd saved up enough money to last me a few months, knowing that the day would come when I would reach my limit and quit in a blaze of glory. I tended to do that on occasion. But being fired by Blaine Dowd . . . My pride wouldn't stand for that.

"Okay, Blaine," I said. My palms were placed flat on the desk, and I stared him straight in the face. "I've got two words for you, and I want you to remember them, because I promise as God is my witness they will haunt you to the end of your days."

Blaine gulped. Visibly. Audibly. Like Alfalfa on *The Little Rascals*. "What . . . what two words?"

I leaned in closer. "Walter Briggs."

His eyes darted from side to side. "Walter Briggs? The janitor?"

"The janitor's name is Bob, you dumb-ass." I grabbed his yellow sticky note pad, scratched "Walter Briggs" on it, and slapped the note on his desk.

"Walter Briggs," I said slowly, "is my lawyer. You'll be hearing from him soon."

I turned and stormed out of the office, not bothering to

gather my things. I could swear I heard a collective sigh of relief as the door closed behind me.

$$\infty$$

I slammed my front door and kicked off my shoes, then made a beeline for the kitchen, searching through the cabinets until I found my bottle of Scotch. My father had given it to me for my thirtieth birthday, even though he knew I didn't drink hard liquor.

"Everyone has days for which the only cure is Scotch," the card had said. "Just wanted to make sure you were prepared." I opened the bottle.

Good old Dad.

I lay down flat on my living room floor, glass in one hand and bottle in the other, staring at the ceiling.

"This is my life." It sounded even worse out loud than it did in my head. I was thirty-two. Thirty-two. I should have been a doctor. Or a CEO. Or a college professor. Something big. Something meaningful. But I went in a different direction, took a path that led to being jobless and lying on the floor of a crappy apartment with a bottle of Scotch by my side, straining to identify phantom music only I could hear. Oh, if only I could get a picture for the Chappaqua High alumni newsletter . . .

The phone rang. I let it ring three more times before rolling over and grabbing the cordless from under the sofa.

"Leave me alone."

"You fucking bitch." George's voice was rough. *Bitch* came out slurred.

You were right, Dad. Some days definitely call for Scotch.

"George. So good to hear from you." Glancing at the calendar, I confirmed my suspicion. Payday. The only predictable thing about George was a hostile call every other Thursday.

"You and your cunt lawyer can fucking kiss my ass." He slurred on *lawyer* and *ass*. I downed a gulp of the Scotch, and after a few moments of choking on flaming burrs, I felt warm and floaty. Nice.

"I only got half my goddamn paycheck," he continued. His voice dropped to a rabid whisper, which I could barely hear over the sounds of the bar in the background. I was pretty sure it was some sort of death threat. It wouldn't be the first.

"George, no one forced you to represent yourself in court." I could hardly feel sorry for him. He fired three lawyers before stumbling into court drunk and representing himself. I hadn't even asked for alimony. The judge was so pissed off at him that she ordered it on her own.

He coughed. A long, hacking cough. I was reminded of the doctor who, ten years ago, told George he'd be dead in eight if he didn't quit smoking. Friggin' quack. At the rate George was going, he was going to outlive us all, cough or no cough.

"How ya feeling there, George?" I asked, swallowing a minor stab of guilt at my fervent wish that he'd drop dead right that minute. I could live with phantom music if God would just take George out. Easy trade.

"I'm gonna come down there, slit your fucking throat, and get my money back." This from the guy who was too lazy to pull the remote control out from under his own ass. Despite the knowledge that my safety thrived in his sloth, my heart still clenched up in fear. Just like old times.

I got up, walked over to the wall unit, and hit the red button on my phone. "Care to say that again, George?"

His behavior in court had been the setup, but the recorded threats were the slam dunk. George caught my drift, added a string of profanities to his greatest hits, and hung up. I poured myself another drink and lay down on the living room floor, thinking about Walter Briggs and his business card and wondering if I'd ever get to like the taste of Scotch.

෨෨

"So . . . so what you're saying is, you'd like for me to sue . . . who, exactly?" Walter loosened his tie and poured himself a glass of water from the pitcher on the table. I'd called him after waking up on the floor the morning after Blaine Dowd had fired me. I told him I wanted to pursue legal action and asked him to meet me at the Fireside Diner. Surprisingly, he agreed.

The Fireside was drastically misnamed, as there was no fire to be found in the place, save the flaming embers on the ends of the cigarettes the waitresses smoked out back by the Dumpsters. It was a cheap little dive with linoleum tables and a rotating dessert cylinder so huge it partially blocked the entrance, but it was within walking distance of my place and I thought the fresh air would do me some good.

I was right. By the time I got there, I felt like I could take on the world. Or at least Walter Briggs.

"I want to sue the city of Hastings, Hastings General Hospital, and Channel 8. Oh, and my ex-husband."

Walter's eyebrows lifted. "Your ex-husband? What did he do?"

"He's alive. I want you to sue him for not being dead yet."

Walter sat back, his white dress shirt sticking a bit to his skin. It's possible the Fireside had been named for the fact that it was always hot as hell in there. "You can't sue for that."

"Why not? He's supposed to be dead by now. Doctor's orders."

Walter laughed, a cue for me to join in and say I was joking. I kept quiet. He stopped laughing. "We can't sue a guy for not being dead."

"Can we sue the doctor who told me he'd croak, then?"

He stared at me for a moment, sizing me up, an unsure smile tugging at his face. "You're serious?"

"Dead serious."

He tapped his pencil on his legal pad. I looked at my watch, raised my hand, and summoned the waitress.

He leaned forward. "Look, you're upset, and I understand, but you asked me for advice and here it is. You can't sue four people at the same time."

"Why not? Is there a law against it?"

He shrugged reluctant acquiescence. "No, but . . ."

"Then I can do it."

He sighed. "Let me rephrase. It's not in your best interest to sue four people at the same time. And I'm also pretty sure that your ex-husband's being alive is not an infringement of your basic civil rights."

I crossed my arms and leaned back in my seat, sizing Walter up.

"I don't get you," I said finally. "You're a lawyer. The more people I sue, the more money you make. So what's your problem?"

"Maybe I'm not about the money."

"Everybody's about the money," I said, raising a cynical eyebrow at him. "Especially lawyers."

His face darkened a bit. "Don't get me wrong. I cash my checks like everybody else. But sometimes . . ." He leaned forward and smiled slightly, though the gesture didn't mask the irritation behind his eyes. "Sometimes it's about undoing things that were done wrong. And there are one or two lawyers left who still believe that."

He sat back, looking a little too self-satisfied for my taste. I jerked my chin toward him, careful to maintain the smirk on my face lest he think his little speech got to me. "And I take it you're the one or two, Mr. Do-Right?"

"I'll let you figure that on your own," he said. "You seem the type who likes to do her own thinking."

I raised my eyebrows at him. "You weren't this tough when we first met, Mr. Briggs."

"I adapt to my surroundings, Ms. Lane." His eyes were smiling now, sending me the clear message that he had my number. He didn't seem like your standard ambulance chaser, and I had to admit I was intrigued. I felt a lurch in my gut that had historically led to nothing but trouble, and in an instant I found myself smiling at Walter Briggs.

The waitress arrived, her hip jutted out as though she'd

been born waiting on tables. Her hair was so thick with Aqua Net that if a nuclear bomb were to hit Hastings, Tennessee, there would be nothing left but the militia shelters and a floating platinum-blonde tumbleweed. Grateful for the distraction from the enigmatic Walter Briggs, I turned my smile on her.

"Could you get me a Scotch and water on ice, please? Need a little hair of the dog, if you know what I mean."

She smiled. She knew. "I would, honey," she said, her drawl lingering, "but we don't serve alcohol before noon."

I grinned and held up my watch for her. She glanced at it, then looked up and squinted at the clock. "Well, I'll be damned." She turned and headed to the bar, hips jutting all over the place.

"I like her," I said, turning back to Walter. "If they get air-conditioning here, I might even come back. So what do you say, Counselor?"

"About the diner?" he asked, looking around. "It's okay."

"No, about my lawsuits."

"Ah. Yes." He sat back in his seat and looked at me. There was a long moment of silence, and a slight smile on his lips that projected an air of confidence and security despite his sticky dress shirt. I was beginning to feel like the playground bully who'd just met her match. "I think you might have a case. Maybe two."

"Okay. Where do we start?"

"You've got a decent complaint against Channel 8 for wrongful termination, but the payoff isn't great for all the time and money that go into it. My understanding is the station isn't doing all that well." The waitress brought my drink and I took

it, but my eyes never left Walter. He glanced up briefly to
ensure that he had my attention, and continued.

"I think suing the city of Hastings for negligence is your
best bet. It's a lot of work, but it's likely they'll settle just to keep
it out of the papers." He scribbled on his legal pad. He was left-
handed. It may be dextrist of me, but I think left-handed people are more trustworthy. I myself am right-handed. "As for
Hastings General Hospital . . . what's wrong with you exactly?"

"I hear music."

He gave that bobbing nod people gave you when they had
no idea what you were talking about. "You hear music."

"Phantom music. Ever since the injury." I held my hands
up, requesting silence. Walter leaned forward, as though he
were listening for the music in my head. I sat back. "I can't hear
it at the moment. It comes and goes."

He sat back as well. "Okay."

"And I'm not crazy."

"I didn't say you were."

"But you were thinking it."

"You don't know what I'm thinking."

"Oh, please. If you told me you were hearing phantom
music no one else could hear, I'd think you were crazy."

"Good thing you're not me, then."

Well, shut me up. I took another sip of my Scotch.

"Where are you from?" I asked. "Not from around here."

"No." He looked at me, his enjoyment of my irritation clear
in his eyes.

"Well?"

"Well, what?" He smiled. He knew damn well what.

"You're from up East, aren't you?"

His smile broadened. "How'd you know?"

"Because conversationally, you're a pain in the ass."

"Well, that makes two of us."

I huffed. "Fine. Chappaqua, New York."

He nodded. "Newton, Massachusetts."

I took another drink. I'd earned it. Walter's smile played on his lips a moment longer before he spoke again.

"Phantom music," he said, looking at me. He'd put down his legal pad. "And how is that the hospital's fault?"

"It's not." I took a sip of my Scotch. The drink was still mighty foul, but I was beginning to appreciate its effects. And I'd found that the more I drank, the less I disliked it. "It's just that they didn't do anything about it. Basically, they flashed a light in my ears, said it wasn't tinnitus, gave me a bill, and booted me out. I can sue for that, can't I?"

Walter tapped his pencil against the table but kept his eyes locked on me. "I don't think so."

His eyes had subtle smile crinkles around the edges; I read them as indicating a healthy sense of humor but not an over-bearing cheerfulness. My stomach lurched again, making me feel vulnerable and off balance. I adjusted myself to sit up straighter and went into attack mode, which was traditionally my response when I found myself attracted to someone.

Drive them away. *Fast.*

I met his gaze and raised him an eyebrow. "So what's your deal, Walter Briggs?"

"What do you mean, Wanda Lane?" Smile. Lurch.

Attack.

"I mean the nurse told me you were at my bedside every day during the coma. She even thought you were my boyfriend." I could see his confidence deflate a little, but he maintained eye contact. "I can't figure out why someone I don't know would sit by my bedside for five days."

Walter shrugged. "I heard about what happened at the courthouse. I thought you had a case."

"Against the city of Hastings."

He nodded. "Yes."

"So you visited me every day for five days so you could drop off your business card?"

"Pretty much. Yes."

I crossed my arms and sat back, eyeing him sharply. "Even an ambulance chaser wouldn't be that desperate for work, and you don't look desperate. So what gives?"

"I'm not an ambulance chaser," he said, shifting in his seat. "I'm a civil attorney."

"Exactly. So what gives?"

He sighed and stared at me, his mouth clamped shut.

"Have you ever sat by an accident victim's bed for five days before?" I prodded. I saw a flash in his eyes, but it passed.

"Not to get a case, no," he said thickly.

"Then I still don't understand why you were there."

He sighed and sat back. "I was in the courthouse that day. I heard what happened. I knew there was no padding under the carpeting, which would have minimized your injuries. I had another client in the hospital, so I stopped in to check up on you when I was visiting him."

He kept his eyes locked on mine as he spoke, and his composure was steely, but I still knew he was lying, or at least not telling the whole truth. I'd accomplished my goal of toppling his balance, however, and I wasn't in the mood to beat the whole story out of him, so I held up my drink and waved at Tumbleweed, giving the international sign for "Make it two."

Walter let loose with a subtle smile. "I usually don't drink during the day."

"Well, Walter," I said, "if you're going to be hanging out with me, you're gonna need a drink."

👁👁

When I was sixteen, I lost my virginity to a guy who went by the nickname of Shooter. We were in the back of his pickup truck, which was parked in the lot of the elementary school. It was ten-thirty at night. We'd just gotten off a shift working at the local grocery store, where I was a cashier and he was a stock boy, and had gone for a drive. I was crazy about him, and he was crazy about getting some, and before I got my jeans buttoned up again, he was revving up the engine and ready to drive home. He was halfway to his own house before I got over my humiliation enough to remind him that I was still in the car with him. At first, he didn't get my drift, so I explained that my car was back at the store, and I'd need to be getting home sometime that evening. He dropped me off at my car and didn't speak to me again until about seven years later, when he called me out of the blue, apologizing.

It was one of his twelve steps.

My point is, I'm great at witty repartee and I'm a hell of a dancer, but when it comes to important life decisions, I'm dumber than dirt. Which was why, two seconds after entering my apartment from lunch with Walter, I rushed back outside to wave his car down and tell him I didn't really want to sue anyone.

By the time I got outside, all I could see were the taillights on Walter's Chevy Blazer disappearing from sight as he turned from Carmella Street onto Pine. I trudged back up into my apartment and called him on his cell phone.

"Walter Briggs."

"Yeah, Walter, it's me. Look, forget the whole thing. Forget the lawsuits. I'm just . . . you know, I'm not thinking straight. Too much Scotch. Too little sleep. Good thing you were driving, huh?" I gave an insipid little giggle and punched myself on the leg to make it stop. I sounded like an idiot. Like a schoolgirl. I could feel the upper hand I'd gained at lunch slipping like wet rope through my hands.

"Wanda?" His voice crackled through. "I can't hear you. Look, I'm gonna turn around. I'll be at your place in a minute."

Click. I put the phone down on the counter and backed away from it slowly as though it were a snake. Somehow, right then, I knew that I was going to sleep with Walter when he walked through the door. What I didn't know was whether that was going to be a decision I'd simply regret, like sleeping with Shooter, or a decision that would haunt me for the rest of my days, like marrying George. I ran to the bathroom to brush my teeth. Either way, I was gonna need fresh breath.

ဖ

Walter's finger was barely off the buzzer before I had the door open. He stepped into the apartment and I shut the door behind him. I smiled at him. He smiled back, the right corner of his mouth creeping up faster than the left, and there was a hint of curiosity in his expression. Couldn't say as I blamed him. I wasn't exactly an easy read.

He looked around and rocked back on his heels for a second, waiting on me. I said nothing. Finally, he spoke. "You *did* call me, right?"

I nodded. "Yes." I was starting to feel a little dizzy. I put my hand on his shoulder for some balance. It was a nice, firm shoulder. Wasn't expecting that. A guy in a suit and tie had no business being all taut underneath. My hand flew back to my side as though it had been burned, the tingling in my fingers cementing the impression.

Walter's eyebrows furrowed. "Are you okay?"

No. I felt disoriented. And unbelievably turned on. If he smiled at me again, I'd melt right there into a puddle at his feet. Not a position of power, that. He put his hands on my shoulders and guided me to a seat in the recliner behind me.

"I'll be right back," he said. I said nothing, but my internal critic was chanting *Idiot, idiot, idiot* at me.

Walter returned with a glass of water. He handed it to me, kneeling beside me as I drank it. I put it down on the coffee table. He put his hand on mine and smiled at me. "Feel better?"

His eyes smiled on mine. *Lurch.* Between the Scotch wearing down the parts of my brain that knew better and the knowledge that Walter would soon be leaving me alone in that damn apartment again if I didn't give him a reason to stay, I felt a certain desperation to kick it up a notch. I pushed myself forward until our faces collided into a kiss. At first, it was awkward, as though our heads were a couple of balls that knocked into each other in a high school gym, but after a moment, when realization of a mistake should have parted us, it was still going. The groove was on.

We parted on the same beat and looked at each other, our eyes searching, scanning, wondering. *Did I just have my tongue in this person's mouth? Did what I think just happened actually just happen? Am I—maybe, please, oh God please—about to have sex?*

Then Walter sprang up, and the groove came to a screeching halt. He paced for a few steps, then turned to me and held out his arms like a crossing guard warning me to stay put. "Um, that's not why I came over here."

"Okay," I said. "What's your point?"

"I owe you an apology."

I stared at him. "Why?"

He stood up and backed away a bit. "Because this looks like I got you drunk and came back to take advantage of you."

I rolled my eyes. Just what I needed. A friggin' gentleman. "But I called you."

He nodded, appraising that evidence. "Yes, you did."

"Then I kissed you."

He shrugged and nodded but made a gesture of dismissal with his hand, as though he would have kissed me if I hadn't kissed him first. I liked that. It was like getting a little bit of dignity on a platter. I stood up and moved closer, hoping that proximity would realign the groove. "So what's the problem?"

Walter looked at my sofa, my coffee table, my feet. Anything but my eyes. "Well . . ."

I put my hand on his chin and turned his head until his eyes met mine. I smiled. He smiled. I licked my lips. His eyes did a half-closed flutter thing, and I could hear his breath come faster. I started unbuttoning my shirt. He grabbed my hand to stop me right as I was fiddling with the button of no return.

"Wanda, stop."

"Why?" I said in a husky whisper. I put my hand on the back of his neck and pulled him in for a kiss, which he entertained for a moment before pulling away.

"Wanda." He put his hands on my shoulders and held me back. "I don't want to do this."

"Coulda fooled me." I reached down and gently grabbed the evidence that he was glad to see me. He yelled and jumped back about five feet, knocking into the wall behind him and setting my framed Ansel Adams print into a determined tilt.

"Guess I misunderstood," I said, angrily buttoning my shirt. "My apologies."

"Wanda, don't be hurt." He reached to put his hand on my arm, but I wrenched myself away.

"I'm not hurt, I'm horny." I stared him in the eye as I buttoned the last button, then reached for my jacket, fumbling in the pockets. "And now I'm frustrated and I need a cigarette."

"You shouldn't smoke."

"You're not my lawyer and you're not my lover, Walter. You

don't get to tell me what to do." I pulled a cigarette out of my pack and went back into my pockets for the lighter. I didn't smoke very often but always had a pack handy, just in case something humiliating happened and I needed a quick fix of *I don't give a shit.*

Walter held up his hands. "Sorry. You're right. None of my business."

I pulled the cigarette from my lips and gestured toward him with it. "What's your deal, Walter? You gay or something?"

"No, I'm not gay." He rubbed his fingers over his forehead. "This is not going well."

"So, what, then? Married? Confused? Bitter? Considering the priesthood? What?" I snagged the lighter and turned my back on him, heading toward the front door. He followed me outside, closing the door behind us as I lit up.

"It's not any of that," he said softly. "It's just that I . . . You surprised me. That's all."

"I surprised you." I took a drag. "I see."

There was silence for a short while as we both watched my exhaled smoke dissipate into the air. Although it wasn't the best area of town, the view of Hastings from my balcony was pretty decent. The white haze that hovered over the town from the flour factory made it seem like a white city, its purity almost palpable, if you were naive enough to believe in purity.

I was almost done with my cigarette by the time Walter spoke again. "You don't want to sue anybody, then?"

I shook my head. "No."

"Okay." He took a step away, then stopped, then moved a little, then stopped. I took another drag of my cigarette. "Look, I wish . . ."

He paused. I never knew what he was going to say, because he turned and left before he could finish.

3

It was just me and Albert, my bottle of Chivas Regal, for most of the following week. Actually, it was several bottles of Chivas, but I just named them all Albert. Hell, it worked for the Lassie people, it could work for me.

I drank and watched Fox News Channel until I almost turned Republican. Then I watched CNN until I almost turned stupid.

On Wednesday of that week, I was watching Animal Planet.

On Friday, I looked in the mirror and decided that there's a reason why people were discouraged from staying in dark apartments and drinking for days at a stretch. My eyes were red-rimmed and half-closed, and my skin was downright sallow.

I looked like hell.

It was also on Friday that I got a call from Faye Whittle. Faye "I'm so sorry you got blown up" Whittle. Fay "I'll give you half of my settlement if you testify" Whittle. Faye "I'd never screw you out of your money right after you've lost your job" Whittle.

Okay, so she never actually said that last one, but she implied it.

"The settlement wasn't as much as I'd hoped," she said. I could practically hear the deed being signed on her beach home as we spoke.

"I'm fine, Faye, thanks for asking."

She sighed into the phone. "Once I pay for lawyer's fees and all, it's really nothing."

"I'll take half of nothing."

"Oh, Wanda!" She laughed. "I couldn't give you half! Remember, it was my business that got destroyed, my livelihood."

"Yeah, and it was my ass that got blown up while you were at the 7-Eleven getting yourself a cherry Slurpee." I hadn't found out about that until recently, and I'd been dying to use it against her. It was almost worth losing the money to say it aloud.

"I needed change to call the gas company!" she squealed as I hung up the phone.

I walked over to the base on the wall and turned off the machine. The phantom music started up, and I turned up the volume on the television, then went into the kitchen to stare into the fridge, as I did every evening at around seven o'clock.

The week had been bad. I'd eaten from cans and boxes for most of it, and now my refrigerator had only some cranberry sauce in a small Tupperware bowl and a jar of green olives I couldn't recall buying. A person's food store says a lot about him or her, and what mine was saying about me was damn depressing.

Staring at my paltry refrigerator reminded me of a girl in my freshman dorm named Debbie Manney who used to look on the bright side of everything. Debbie would have told me that my empty fridge was a sign of a new beginning, a fresh start, a call to action to reinvent myself by purchasing rare and wonderful food items, like cilantro and pomegranates.

I hated Debbie Manney.

I had been friendly to her, though. You couldn't *not* be friendly to Debbie Manney. That would be like kicking the pope. So I tolerated her squeaky presence long enough for her to leave her indelible mark of sunshine on my tender psyche. When Mike Benedetto dumped me and then asked me to loan him my car so he could take Mary Ann Sheeley to his frat's social, Debbie sat with me all night and braided my hair while I ate Ben & Jerry's Cherry Garcia. She said that depression was a valuable tool, that without it we would never appreciate the good times.

"You can't enjoy the sunshine if you've never been in the dark," she'd said. I think I hated her so much simply because there was nothing to hate about her. She was cute. She was sweet. She was balanced. She did yoga. She planned to wait until her wedding night and never thought twice about it. She was a freak.

Last I heard, Debbie was living a fulfilled life as a stay-at-home mom with her two sons and wonderful husband somewhere near Syracuse, New York. Anytime I got news of how she was doing, I nodded and smiled, but deep inside, I convinced myself she hid flasks of Absolut Citron in her purse and had regular dalliances with the pizza guy. It was vicious and bitter, admittedly, but it got me through the day.

As I sat on my living room floor, watching Fox News and clutching Albert to my side, I thought about Debbie, and it occurred to me for the first time that she might actually be happy. She might have figured it out. She might be someplace that no one I'd ever known had found. She might be on the wagon. She might never have been off the wagon. The possibility occurred to me, for a brief moment, that it might be actually attainable, this sense of purpose and fulfillment that Dr. Phil and Oprah kept talking about.

And then Bill O'Reilly came on, and I realized the whole world was a bottomless pit of crap, just like I'd always known.

There was a pounding on my door on Saturday morning. Early Saturday morning.

Eight a.m., in fact.

"Wanda!" The voice was muted through the front door, but I could still hear it, because I had fallen asleep on the doormat.

"Wanda!" Ring. Ring. Knock-knock-knock.

"Go awaaaayyyy," I mumbled into the doormat, but the door pounding continued, in perfect time with the hammering in my head. I grabbed the doorknob, pulled myself up, and put my eye to the peephole.

Walter. Good friggin' God.

I opened the door, leaving the chain on and wedging my face into the four inches of open space. "Whaaaaaat!?" I groaned.

"You haven't been answering your phone," he said. He

sounded worried. I couldn't tell how he looked because my eyes wouldn't open.

"I'm fine."

There was a pause, then a firm "Open the goddamn door."

One of the bonuses of having a calm personality is that you can pull out the occasional "goddamn" and get instant results. Not the case with hotheads like myself. I stepped back, forced my eyes open, and released the chain. Walter was inside in a flash, with his hands on my shoulders, looking at my face.

"You're sure you're okay? You look like hell."

"Thanks a lot," I said, stepping away from him and heading over to the kitchen counter, where I sat on a barstool and rested my head against the cool Formica. "What are you doing here?"

"You haven't been answering your phone."

"Why were you calling me?" I asked. My voice was hoarse, and my throat hurt. Friggin' Albert. I knew he'd turn on me.

Walter opened the living room window and flicked on the kitchen light. Ouch. "This place smells funny."

"Probably because I haven't left it for five days."

There was a moment of silence, then his hands hooked under my armpits and lifted me off the stool. By the time I opened my eyes, I was in my shower, still in my pajamas, with cold water beating down on my back.

"Clean up. I'll be in the living room when you're done."

I cursed him out from the shower, but by the time I stumbled back into my living room, I was appreciating clean clothes and a freshly washed body like a born-again Christian appreciates Jesus.

My living room was cleaner than it was when I'd left it, and

I inhaled the resuscitating scent of fresh-brewed coffee. Walter was putting the last dish into the dishwasher and wiping down the kitchen sink when I settled onto one of my barstools.

"Thank you," I said. I wasn't sure he had heard it, but I caught a slight nod as he wiped my kitchen counter and threw the sponge into the sink. He poured two mugs of black coffee and pushed one toward me. There was silence for a long time, and just when I was about to pipe in with a wiseass comment, he spoke.

"My wife died."

I looked up at him, but he was staring into his mug.

"Excuse me?" I said, working a decent amount of indignation into my voice. Internally, I was recoiling at the idea that I'd grabbed the business end of a married man. I did have my limits, and breaking up marriages was one of them. I opened my mouth to hurl the appropriate invective at him when he spoke again.

"Six years ago. She was hit by a car, crossing the street to get the mail." His voice cracked a bit. I was starting to understand. My heart sank. The indignation disappeared. "She was in a coma for eight weeks."

He looked up. His eyes were dry, steely. "I sat by her bedside every day. The doctors asked me to make a decision. They told me there was no hope. It took me eight weeks to believe them, and a day hasn't gone by when I haven't regretted it."

I could feel heat in my throat, but I said nothing. What could I say? *Gee, I'm sorry? Boy, that sucks?* The last thing a guy like that needed was my sympathy. Or me, for that matter.

"I was on my way out from visiting a client when I walked by your room at Hastings General." Walter took one sip of his coffee, then put the mug down so carefully that it didn't make a sound. "You were alone."

I remained silent. If I spoke, I'd cry. How pathetic I must have seemed in that hospital all by myself. The idea that Walter was some creep hoping to cop a feel off a comatose chick was far less painful than the reality that he was a good guy who had taken pity on me.

"Her name was Maggie." I could tell he was looking at me, waiting for me to make eye contact, but I just stared into my coffee mug, wishing it were big enough for me to dive into and drown myself. "I just wanted you to know that I'm not a psycho or a creep. I'm not a freak who can't get over his wife's death. I'm just a regular guy who probably made a mistake."

What mistake? I wanted to ask. *Sitting by my side? Going to lunch with me? Kissing me? All of the above?*

"This isn't the way my life is supposed to be," I said, my head jolting up in a "Who said that? Did I say that?" motion.

Walter shrugged and smiled. Kindly. Pitying me. Again. He reached over and put his hand gently on my cheek. It was warm and soft, and the energy from his palm made my face tingle. "Then change it."

And he left.

Twenty minutes later I left to hit the 7-Eleven, get a cherry Slurpee, and check out the want ads.

ᎧᎧ

I grabbed a red pen from the mug on the counter and sat down at the kitchen table with my Slurpee. I circled an ad for a parts supervisor at a local Mazda dealership. I circled another one for a dental hygienist. I even circled an ad trying to sell a 1973 Nova before I realized I wasn't really paying attention.

I was thinking about Walter. I was seeing the look on his face when he talked about his wife. I was seeing him sitting by her bed in the hospital. I was imagining how happy they were when they first got married. Like every story with a tragic ending, the beginning and middle become flawless by comparison. In my mind, no two people had ever been happier and no two people had ever suffered a greater tragedy, although I knew that in reality she probably got pissed off at him every Friday when he forgot to take the garbage out, and he probably hated the way she picked her teeth after eating movie popcorn.

I shook my head and tried to concentrate on the want ads, flipping back to the beginning. My red pen was hovering over the paper, ready to strike at the perfect job, when I saw it.

Do something meaningful.

That was it. The entire ad. "Do something meaningful."

I sat with my mouth agape. Do something *meaningful*?

I felt the anger flame out from my gut. Who the hell did this guy think he was? *Do something meaningful*? What, like people who are unemployed are all losers? Their lives have no meaning? They have no purpose in the world? That's exactly what the unemployed need—some friggin' self-righteous bastard putting something like that in the friggin' want ads.

"Do something meaningful," I muttered to myself as I dialed the sales line for the classified ad department. "I'll give you meaningful. Bite me. How's that? Meaningful enough for you?"

"*Hastings Daily Reporter*, this is Jennifer. Can I interest you in a personals ad, four lines for four dollars for the first week?"

"No. But thanks. Hey, look, there's an ad in this week's employment pages, and I want to know who placed it." The red pen cap clenched in my teeth marred my speech. I spit it out. It bounced across the kitchen counter and landed in the sink.

"It doesn't say in the ad? Usually, the business will put their number in the ad?" Jennifer was one of those southern belles who pronounced her sentences like they were questions. I imagined her with curly red hair all pulled back in an adorable little pony-tail that looked good no matter how quickly she had to jump up out of bed in the morning, and decided to hate her on principle.

"Yeah. I know. But this doesn't have a number. It just says, 'Do something meaningful.'" I sipped loudly on my Slurpee.

"That's in the employment pages?"

"Yes, it is, and I'd like to lodge a complaint."

"A complaint? Why? It sounds kind of nice to me."

"Well, you have a job, don't you, Jennifer?" She paused. Point taken. "Is there anyone there I can complain to? Do you have a supervisor or something? Can you track down the sorry bastard who placed that ad and beat him senseless for me?"

"Well . . . no. Yes. And no. But I don't think complaining to my supervisor would help much? There's really not much we can do; once an ad is placed, it's placed? If it helps, I think that ad was meant for the personals? There's a person who does that every now and again, places a nice message in the personals, you know, just to be inspirational? I think it's kind of nice?"

I could feel my teeth grinding with every lilt at the end of her sentences. I tapped my red pen against the counter. "Fine. Then, can I place an ad?"

"Personals. Four lines for four dollars for the first week."

"Okay. Do this for me. 'Dear Meaningful: Who the hell do you think you are? Wanda wants to know. 555-8936.'"

I could hear Jennifer typing. She read the message back to me. "Now, we're gonna need your credit card?"

"Fine," I said, grabbing my purse.

"That'll be a total of fifty-six dollars?"

I stopped rifling through my purse. "Fifty-six dollars? What was that four-dollar crap you just quoted me?"

"Oh, that's four dollars for the first week? With a three-week minimum? Each additional week is twenty-six dollars?"

"For crying out loud, you people have no shame."

"Do you have that credit card?"

"Not for fifty-six dollars, I don't."

She sighed. "Okay, tell you what? I'll shave it down to two lines, use a smaller font and such, we'll run it for two weeks, I can do it for . . . twenty-two dollars?"

I stared at the ad. *Do something meaningful.* Was I furious enough at this bastard to charge twenty-two dollars to a card with an interest rate of prime plus 5 percent? Did I really want him to call me just so I could ream him a new one? Was I really such an angry, petty person as to waste my time on relatively fruitless pursuits?

Absolutely. "Ready for that card number, Jennifer?"

The thing about sitting home being unemployed was that I was horribly bored and yet too depressed to do anything. I should have been out volunteering my time to the homeless, or the foodless, or the shameless. Something. Instead, I sat on the sofa with the remote control making imprints in my flesh, flipping between eight million varieties of crappy cable programming, playing them loudly to drown out the phantom music that hovered overhead, waiting for an opportunity to strike.

This isn't how my life is supposed to be. I cringed every time I heard myself say it, shuddered at the memory of the look on Walter's face. He felt sorry for me. There was only one thing I hated more than being the object of someone's pity, and I was too consumed with self-loathing to even remember what that was.

I would have gotten up and called the Mazda dealership, wooed them into hiring me with my "Go get 'em" grin, but the very thought of selling a replacement side-view mirror for a hundred and seventeen dollars only depressed me more. So I continued my interim occupation as a cable commando. It was me, Lucy, Ricky, Cousteau, and that guy with the sweaters hawking Amazing Crap You Just Can't Live Without.

I was a few days into my self-pity wallow when the phone rang. I answered it instantly, not caring who it was. Even if it was George, it would at least keep me from ordering a Rocket Chef.

Her voice was frail. Tired. Wispy. "Hi, I'm calling about your ad."

I hit the mute on the remote and shut up Sweater Guy.

"My ad?" I scanned my brain for anything relating to placing an ad and came up dry. Albert was hell on short-term memory.

"Yeah. Um . . . I'm Laura."

Laura. She sounded quiet. And a little sad. My mind raced. My ad, my ad . . .

My ad.

My indignation raged anew for a brief moment as I remembered the offense. "That was you?" I asked, hardly believing it. She didn't sound like the self-righteous type. As a matter of fact, she sounded like someone who was desperate for any human contact that might prevent her from ordering a Rocket Chef from the Amazing Sweater Guy.

"I'm sorry?" she said. Sounded like a question. Just like Jennifer. Friggin' southern belles. But it worked. My anger deflated. That was all I wanted, a simple apology.

And that's what I got.

"Look, don't worry about it. Just think about it before you do something like that again, okay?"

I hung up and tossed the phone into the corner with my pile of dirty laundry and turned the sound back on the television. Amazing Sweater Guy was gone, replaced by someone selling spray-on hair color, and the world was once again proven perilous for idiots with disposable cash.

♋

I'm in a rowboat with three babies and a pig, none of which are mine, but all of which are looking to me to do something. I'm wearing my prom dress and a pair of really cute, strappy black shoes. I'm rowing, trying to save the lot of us, but despite the fact that we're about ten feet from land, I can't get us there. I try to reach the oar out and sink it into the beach and drag us in, but the boat stays where it is. The pig starts to bite one of the babies, and then the lot of them disappears. In their place sits Bruce Willis. Well, if you want to be technical, David Addison, Bruce's character from *Moonlighting*. There has never been nor shall there ever be a man, fictitious or otherwise, as luscious as David Addison.

Suddenly, I'm not so anxious to get out of the boat.

"Get out," Dave says.

"How?" I whine.

Dave rolls his eyes. He seems angry. I'm annoyed. All I want is a little Motown and some dream time shimmy, and Addison is giving me attitude.

"Step out of the boat. Your feet will get wet, but you'll survive."

I look at the beach. It's pretty, all palm trees and golden sand. But no one's there. It looks lonely. I turn back to Dave.

"What am I going to do when I get there?"

He smiles at me. Now, that's the Addison I know and love. He takes my hand in his. I sigh. I know I'll be hearing some Temptations soon. I lean forward, smiling and waiting for a kiss from a fictional man, which, as everyone knows, are the best kind.

Suddenly, the boat tips over and I'm flat on my ass in a foot of water with various marine nastiness slurping around my ankles. Dave stands in the boat, arms crossed in front of him, stern face glaring down at me. Now he's starting to look more like my dad.

"This isn't how my life was supposed to be," I say, sounding as pathetic as I feel.

"Then change it," he says, and disappears, taking the boat with him, leaving me alone wading in oceanic gunk and wondering how I will ever replace my cute, strappy black shoes.

My alarm went off, roaring at me with AM talk radio. I sat up in bed and looked around. My Exercycle was invisible beneath a mound of laundry. More dirty clothes gathered in clumps, which had taken over my bedroom and were casting greedy glances toward the hallway. The edge of the plate I'd eaten pizza off of last week was peeking out at me from behind the veil of the navy-blue sheets that hung over the side of my bed. My toothbrush was on the carpet next to my closet, lying beside an empty bottle of Albert.

"So this is what rock bottom looks like," I grumbled as I got out of bed.

I started with the windows, pulling the shades up and yanking them all open as far as they would go. The fresh air was a start, but there were only three windows in the whole place, so I had to leave the door wide open to get any sort of cross-breeze. I put a red bandanna over my hair and slipped a Motown CD in the stereo, letting the Supremes tell me how it is.

The apartment was passably clean by noon, and I was hearing it through the grapevine when I felt a hand on my shoulder. I screamed and whirled around, banging the CD player off the kitchen counter. My heart jumped out of my body and hightailed it out the door, bouncing down the stairs and jumping over the fire hydrant on its way to someplace sane. The rest of me stood with my hand over the hollow space in my chest, trying to regain my breath as Walter Briggs looked down at me, his face soft with amusement.

"Sorry," he said. He didn't look terribly sorry to me. "I knocked. Your music was too loud. I could have been a psychopath, you know."

I raised an eyebrow. "Who says you're not?"

He saw my eyebrow and raised me a grin. "Only time will tell."

We held each other's eyes for a moment. My heart leaped back into my chest and did a wild tap dance for a few beats before I dropped my eyes, losing the game of romantic chicken.

"The place looks good. Definitely smells better." He turned back and grinned at me. "Wish I could say the same for you."

"Bite me, Briggs." And my mother thought that charm school money had been wasted. I walked over to the fridge and pulled out a pitcher of freshly made iced tea. "Want some?"

He eyed me suspiciously. "Is there alcohol in it?"

"No. I'm on the wagon for the moment."

"Glad to hear it." He grinned and my heart gave another little tap. *Ba-doo-boom-chaaaa.* I busied myself pouring two glasses of tea and leaned over the counter in my best pseudo-seductive stance, then caught a glance of my reflection, wearing an old Huey Lewis concert T-shirt and black sweats, in the mirror by the front door. I also caught a whiff of Lysol and Scotch. I leaned back. There would be no seduction today, pseudo or otherwise.

"What brings you here?" I asked. "Am I being sued?"

"Not unless you know something I don't." He pulled an envelope out of his coat pocket and placed it on the counter. "Actually, I'm making a delivery."

I gave him a curious look and opened the envelope. In it was a check made out to me for ten thousand dollars, signed by Edgar Dowd. I sucked in more air than my lungs could handle and dropped the check back on the counter, taking a few steps back.

Walter laughed. "It's a check, not a snake."

"How . . . ?" I looked up at him. "How did you . . . ?"

He held up his hands. "Don't blame me. You're the one who mentioned my name to Blaine, or so the story goes."

I nodded and recalled stabbing Walter's name onto a sticky note for Blaine. "Yeah. That was me."

"Well, Blaine mentioned it to his dad, and Edgar Dowd came busting into my office this morning, talking about countersuits and getting me disbarred, et cetera, et cetera." Walter rolled his eyes, but he looked more amused than annoyed.

I took a sip of my iced tea. "How'd you end up with a check?"

Walter chuckled. "Beats the hell out of me. I just let him rave until he ran out of gas, and he dumped it on my desk before he left. We didn't sign any paperwork, but cashing it would indicate acceptance of a settlement. Since you said you weren't planning to sue, it looks like a win-win to me."

"Are you kidding?" I picked up the check and stared at it. It felt strange in my hand. It was just a piece of paper, but it had weight. I felt jumbled, confused, off balance. Things like this didn't happen to me. I was never the recipient of good fortune unlooked for. Everything I'd received up to this day I'd gotten off stupid choices and a great smile, and most of it had been well deserved or hard-earned, respectively. I put the check down. It was making me dizzy.

Or maybe I was dizzy in the presence of the guy who delivered it. I looked up at Walter and felt my throat clench as my smile grew, and I knew that I was in what my mother would describe as deep doo-doo.

Walter looked up and caught me staring at him. He met my gaze, smiling back. We were silent for a few moments while I fought with myself over what to say and eventually said the very worst thing possible.

"I'm sorry about your wife."

His smile dropped. His jaw tightened. His eyes withdrew. "I'd rather not talk about that."

I held up my hands. "Look, I'm sorry. I just wanted you to know . . ."

"It was a long time ago." He avoided eye contact, and I had to fight the instinct to reach out and touch him. And then the phantom music began. I closed my eyes.

"Are you okay?" Walter's voice blew gently away against the force of the music. Crescendo approaching . . . so close . . .

Gone.

I felt Walter's hand on my arm. "Wanda?"

I opened my eyes. "I'm sorry. Phantom music. I know the tune, but it always goes away before I can place it."

"Are you seeing anyone?" he asked. My heart did another

ba-doo-boom-chaaa until I realized he was speaking of my mental health, not my sexual availability.

"I'm not crazy."

"I never said you were."

I shrugged. Whatever. I picked up the check and waved it in the air. "How much do I owe you?"

Walter shrugged, and I could see the tension ebb. "By my count, nothing. I didn't do anything, I didn't say anything. I'm just a messenger."

He stood up. His gray suit fell in perfect straight lines along his body, and I was picturing the form underneath it before I could stop myself.

"I have to give you something," I said quickly, waving the check again. "I mean, I've been in an office with Edgar Dowd before. The man's certifiable. You deserve to be compensated."

He smiled. *Hoo-wah.*

"I don't need anything. I just wanted to give that to you." He put his hand on my shoulder and squeezed, the kind of awkward gesture a Pee Wee football coach gives to the runt he wouldn't put on the field. "I have to go. Just thought you could use that. Thought it might give you a little breathing room. You know, while you look for a job."

Ouch. I could see a slight flinch when he realized he probably shouldn't mention my employment, or lack thereof. The same way I shouldn't have mentioned his wife. We were in a dead heat for Most Awkward Moments in a Single Conversation. I pasted on a smile. "Thank you."

He was gone a moment later, and I was standing in the middle of my living room, holding ten thousand dollars and having no idea which foot to step with first. Then the phone rang. I grabbed it off the counter, still staring out the open door where Walter had just been.

"I'm calling about the ad." The voice was male. Husky. Sounded like the kind of guy who puts up drywall.

"Ad?" I was confused. This definitely wasn't Laura, who had already called, confessed, and been forgiven. The case was closed.

"Yeah, from the paper? Is this Wanda?"

"Yes, this is Wanda, but . . ." Maybe Laura had been calling about the wrong ad. Or this guy was. Maybe everyone in Hastings was dyslexic. Maybe I shouldn't have paid for two weeks. I cleared my throat and tried to put some meat into my tone.

"Yeah, this is Wanda. Are you the one . . . ?" I trailed off, distracted by some movement across the street that I thought for a moment might be Walter. I stepped closer to the door and saw it was Manny, my mailman.

"Well, I don't know, baby. Are *you* the one?" He was trying to sound seductive, but the chewing noises, followed by the distinct *patooey* of what I imagined to be a tobacco-laced loogie, kind of ruined the effect. I cringed.

"Ewww," I said, and hung up the phone. Thirty seconds later I was listening to a tinny ringing, waiting for Jennifer to pick up at the *Hastings Daily Reporter*.

"Hi, this is Jennifer with the classifieds department at the *Hastings Daily Reporter?* I'm not here right now, but if you'd leave a message, I'd be glad to call you back?"

I hung up and looked at the clock: 12:47. Catching another whiff of Lysol and Scotch, I tossed the phone on the counter and headed for the shower.

4

"Forgive me, Father, but I'm not Catholic." I blew my nose into the handful of tissues I had been swiping my face with since the crying jag hit. That was the danger of the shower: if your life sucked, you were most likely to take notice when you were naked and wet. Might be the reason why depressed people tended to go so long between showers.

It all started with the damn Ivory soap. I haven't bought Ivory in three years, because it was George's brand and the smell tended to turn my stomach. So why buy it? you ask. Good question. My stupid but honest answer was that I bought it on an internal triple-dog-dare, a game of emotional Russian roulette in the personal hygiene aisle. I did it to prove to myself that I was not going to allow my choice of soap to be dictated by a shitty ex-husband.

It made sense at the time.

The package of Ivory sat in my bathroom while I showered with a dwindling sliver of Dove. A week of Albert was more than the sliver could handle, and so I opened the Ivory, took one whiff, and spent the next thirty minutes curled up in the tub in a fetal position, flooded with vivid memories of the worst years of my life.

Those years started when George and I met in college. Well, I was in college, anyway; he was a bouncer at Pappy's, the bar my friends and I used to frequent. He was ten years older than me, sexy and dangerous, a biker guy with a tenderness hidden deep inside, a tenderness only I could see. The reason I was the only one who could see it, of course, was that it existed only in my imagination, but that's neither here nor there.

Okay, maybe it's a little there.

George used to flirt with me at the door at Pappy's, tease me about my fake ID, make jokes about how tight my ass was. Looking back, I find it mortifying that I was charmed by that. But a nineteen-year-old who memorized facts about Sarasota, Florida, just in case anyone questioned her fake ID was not someone with her finger on the pulse of reality.

George had a motorcycle. He wore leather jackets, and he knew the cousin of the drummer from Whitesnake. He smoked and ate greasy food and drank until he passed out. He had long hair and a beard, and my parents were going to hate him.

In other words, he was perfect. Exciting and dangerous for a start, but then once we got married, he would change and settle down and be an exemplary husband and father, and we would laugh about the old days and how rough around the edges he had been before love changed him.

Yes, I really was that stupid.

Even after he hit me the first time, I still had a Pygmalion-style future in mind. He proposed to me after he broke my arm, and I wept as I said, "Yes," over and over again, just knowing that marriage would change him for good, and he would be the George I knew he could be, and we would spend forever lounging naked on the floor, smelling of Ivory soap and watching our dreams come true before our eyes.

I was right about one thing: my parents did hate him. When I told them George and I were getting married—less than twenty-four hours after I promised over the hospital telephone lines that I'd never see the bastard again—my mother stopped talking to me. My dad cut off most of our communication but occasionally still sent birthday gifts with cards that said things like, "Everyone has days for which the only cure is Scotch." Turned out he knew much more about what my future held than I did.

George had successfully accomplished step one in the *Abusive Shit Heel Handbook*: he separated me from my family. From there, it was a short ride to driving off all my friends. And then when I finally dumped the deadweight, I was alone in Hastings, Tennessee, where the smell of Ivory soap would turn me into a pathetic sobbing fetal mass in a sage-green bathtub.

I managed to complete my shower and get dressed, but I couldn't stop crying. I'd pull it together for a minute, then I'd remember my mother's face when I first told her I was moving to Tennessee with George. I'd get a few solid calming breaths in, and then I'd remember how my father's voice cracked when I called to tell him that George and I were getting married. Dad's last words to me were, "Go ahead and marry that bastard if you want, but don't expect us to watch you throw your life down the shitter." Or words to that effect.

I had thought about calling and telling them about the divorce, but it would have just led to painful silences and unanswered questions like, "If you love me so much, why did you abandon me to an abusive shit?" And who needed crap like that around Thanksgiving?

I hobbled out of the shower and managed to get dressed, pausing whenever the crying became too overpowering. I tried to busy myself with housework, but there wasn't much left to do. As time passed and I couldn't stop crying, I started to panic. What if I never stopped crying? What if I died of dehydration and became nothing more than an annotation in a bathroom reader, wedged between the guy who hiccuped himself to death and the chick who bungee jumped off an eighty-foot bridge with a ninety-five-foot bungee cord?

I had to get out. I had to go somewhere. I had to talk to someone. But there was nowhere for me to go and no one for me to talk to. I could have called Walter, but the idea of being the object of his pity again only made the sobbing worse.

So I went to St. Benedict's and weaseled my way into the confessional.

"You're not Catholic?" The priest's voice was cracked and warm. I couldn't see much of his face through the grate between us, but he sounded old and wise. I hoped he'd live up to that impression.

"No," I said. My sobbing had quieted, but the tears were still flowing. "If you want me to leave . . ."

"No," he said. "That's okay. Is anyone waiting out there?"

"I didn't see anyone else."

He released a soft sigh, sounding slightly disappointed. I briefly considered pulling a Debbie Manney and trying to convince him that the lack of penitents was because he was such a good priest and no one was sinning, but he sounded like the kind of guy who could tell horseshit when he heard it. Besides, it was my understanding that God frowned on blowing smoke at priests.

"Would you like to tell me what's bothering you?" he asked.

"I'm alone." My voice was quivering. I cleared my throat and tried to continue with a stronger tone. "I married a real bad guy a few years ago, and he drove my family and friends away."

There was a pause. Then, "No, he didn't."

"Huh?" I wasn't expecting to catch interference from the father.

"He didn't drive your family and friends away. You did."

I leaned closer to the grate. "Do I know you?"

"No," he said. His tone was strong—not accusatory, but not terribly tolerant, either. I got the feeling this wasn't the kind of priest who'd be cutting me a whole lot of slack. "If you chose him, you chose him for a reason. On some level, you wanted to drive your family and friends away, and this guy was probably the most expedient route to that goal. If you want to get over this, you have to take responsibility for those choices."

I felt a flash of fury fly through my gut. "Oh, yeah? I *wanted* to be completely alone and have no one other than a hard-ass priest to talk to?"

He chuckled. "In a nutshell."

I thunked my head on the back of the booth. Now I knew why no one was there. Wednesday was the Day of His Holy Hard-Ass. "Okay," I said through clenched teeth. "Fine."

"Are you angry?" he asked.

"Hell, yeah, I'm angry."

"Good," he said. "We're getting somewhere, then."

I mimicked him silently. Friggin' priests.

After a moment, his voice poked at me through the grate. "Can I tell you what's bothering me?"

This was an unexpected turn of events. I shrugged. "Sure. Why not?"

"I sit here, day in and day out, and listen to people confess. Most of it is small-time stuff. 'I lied about my weight, Father.' 'I had impure thoughts, Father.' 'I wished horrible things would happen to my ex, Father.'"

I shot up. "Is that bad? Is that like a get-into-heaven deal breaker? Because I do that a lot."

He went on, ignoring me. "They have a tally of sins they check off. They come in here and read the list to me. I give them a few Hail Marys and I see them again the next week and it's all the same stuff."

There was a pause. I leaned a little closer to the grate and spoke softly. "Isn't that how it's supposed to work?"

"A little, yes." He sighed. "But most of the real stuff that people do, the things that really hurt them and the people they love, they don't confess to, because they either don't realize they're doing it or they think it's someone else's fault."

I nodded and took a moment to process this before speaking again. "So what you're saying is, George didn't run my family off?"

"No, he didn't."

"So what you're saying is, I'm completely alone in the world because I choose to be?"

"In so many words, yes."

I watched as the tears splashed onto my hands, falling faster as my breathing went all choppy. My voice came out high-pitched and whiny. "This isn't working the way I hoped it would, Father."

"Sometimes what we hope for isn't what's best for us."

I took a moment to gather myself as well as I could. "Okay. Well, I guess I'll be going. Do I need to do anything, a Hail Mary or something?"

"Do you know what a Hail Mary is?"

"No."

I could hear a soft laugh come through the grate. "Then just go out there and do something meaningful to you."

I froze. "What did you say?"

"I said you should do something that has meaning for you."

I half sniffled, half chuckled. "What, is it like National Do Something Meaningful Month or what?"

Another laugh. "I don't know. I don't think so. It doesn't sound like a bad idea, though."

I tucked my tissues in my pocket and rubbed my face with my hands. "Father, what if I can't find anything meaningful to do?"

"Then it will find you."

I nodded, having absolutely no idea what the hell he was talking about. Sure, it sounded like a good priestly answer, but I would have preferred specific instructions, like the kind you get with a bottle of shampoo. Lather. Rinse. Repeat. That I can work with.

I thanked him for his time and pulled back the curtain. There was a woman kneeling in a pew. She crossed herself and stood up, heading toward the booth. I pulled a fresh package of travel-sized tissues out of my jacket pocket and tucked them into her hand.

"You're gonna be needing these," I said, giving her a pat on the shoulder.

"*Hastings Daily Reporter*, this is Jennifer. Can I interest you in a personals ad, four lines for four dollars for the first week?"

"Oh, don't give me that crap, Jennifer." I was trying to pull a sweatshirt over my head with the phone tucked between my ear and my shoulder. I've had better ideas. The phone fell from my grip; when I picked it up, I heard Jennifer's soft southern drawl.

"I'm sorry? Who is this?"

"It's Wanda. Wanda Lane. I called about the 'Do something meaningful' ad. Remember?"

"Oh. Yes." Complete silence. I grabbed the crinkled newspaper off my bed and held it up to the phone. I knew she couldn't see it, but I thought maybe hearing that distinctive newspaper crinkle would put the fear of God into her.

"Yeah," I said. "You wanna tell me what the hell this is?"

Small pause. "I put the ad in for you? Just like you said? In two lines?"

"You said you'd make the font smaller!" I stared at the ad in front of me, which was circled in furious red ink.

"Well, turns out we couldn't do that? So I just edited?"

"Edited?" I shook the newspaper again. In the back of my mind, I knew I looked like a Thorazine candidate, but I went with it. I clutched the paper and read the ad. "'Who are you? Wanda wants to know.' With my phone number! What the hell is that?"

"You said four lines was too expensive? So I edited?"

"It *was* too expensive, you bunch of crooks! But the original request was, 'Who the hell do you think you are?' not 'Who are you?' That's not editing."

I tried to keep my voice even, but it was a task. When I returned from my visit with His Holy Hard-Ass, there were three messages on my machine. I had picked up a paper to continue my job search and listened to the messages as I grazed through the classifieds. I assumed the first message was a wrong number, just some guy rambling about his job. Then there was a woman who said my name and asked if I was a reporter. My eyebrows furrowed and I shook my head, figuring it was time to make my number unlisted, and then I looked back to the classifieds and I saw it.

Then I called Jennifer.

"If you're unhappy with the ad, Ms. Lane, you can write a letter to the paper and we can process a refund."

"Refund! How about you process all the goddamn phone calls I've been getting from people telling me who they are!"

"Have people been calling you? Like who?"

I pulled the phone away from my ear and gave it an "Are you nuts?" look before tossing it back on my shoulder and sputtering, "What?"

"Who's been calling you?"

"Oh, for crying out—I don't know. People. Strangers. Weirdos. Someone named Laura. It's really not the point."

"Maybe it is?" she said. "Maybe this is your chance?"

I was expecting either attitude or acquiescence. Jennifer's conversational, coffee shop tone was throwing me off. "What?"

"Your chance? To do something meaningful?"

"That's it!" I stomped through the apartment, slamming doors for effect. "Take the ad out of the paper. Now!"

"Well, it's too late to stop it for tomorrow, but I can have it out of the paper by . . . Tuesday?"

I breathed through my clenched teeth. "Fine."

"Okay, then? Is there anything else I can help you with today? Are you trying to sell a pet, home furnishing, or car? Because the *Hastings Daily Reporter* has competitive rates—"

I pushed the talk button so forcefully that my thumb hurt, and tossed the phone onto the sofa. I thought briefly about going to the store to get another bottle of Albert, then busted out crying.

My life was a Lifetime movie. I was an out-of-work single woman naming bottles of Scotch, receiving death threats from an abusive ex-husband, and getting phone calls from strangers. They probably wouldn't even be able to get Farrah Fawcett to play me. It'd probably be Kathy Najimy's first dramatic role, and the critics would pan it, saying it's unbelievable that anyone would be as stupid as that Wanda Lane, and then I'd have to move to Tijuana and change my name to Lupe.

And I'd probably still be unemployed.

I sat down on the sofa and leaned my head back, pressing the heels of my hands into my eyes and whining, "My life is a Lifetime movie."

And we all know they only get worse before they get better.

೧౧

The next day started out pretty well, considering how totally fucked it was by 11 a.m. I went to my mailbox promptly at ten for my daily verbal sparring with Manny the Mailman. There are three things in life you can count on: death, taxes, and Manny at ten o'clock.

Manny's a guy in his late fifties from the Bronx. Catholic, with a wife and like fifteen kids and a combative sense of humor. We met at the mailbox not long after I moved into my apartment. He had told me to move my fat ass out of his way; I'd responded that he could move it himself if he didn't mind losing a hand. We've been buds ever since.

"You got a real letter," he said as he handed me my mail with a look of feigned disgust. "I never figured you for the type who had friends."

"Bite me, butthead." It was a lame comeback, but I was more concerned with rifling through the junk to get to the letter. Thoughts of my mother, unrealistic as they were, skirted through my head. She used to write to me when I was in college and even a few letters after George and I moved to

Tennessee. I caught sight of the letter, the familiar chicken scratch etched into the paper with the force of an angry pen, and my stomach turned.

"Who's George?" Manny asked. I didn't respond. "Fucker's got some scary handwriting."

I stared at it. I felt Manny's hand on my shoulder.

"You okay, Wanda?" he asked. For the first time since I'd known him, Manny looked concerned. "You're not breathing."

I inhaled, shrugged his hand off. "Don't touch me, skeeze-ball."

Manny's face fell into a relieved smile, and he continued sorting the mail into the boxes. "They don't pay me enough to deal with people like you."

I wandered back up to my apartment and sat at the counter, the letter lying unopened in front of me until I worked up the courage to reach for the letter opener. George didn't write. George called. I'd gotten only one letter from him in my entire life, and that ended very badly.

I skimmed the letter, then read it more carefully. I paced back and forth in my living room, getting jumpier by the minute. I went into the kitchen, grabbed a bottle of Albert, then put it back. The last thing I wanted was to be drunk when George found me.

When George found me.

Jesus.

I went into the bathroom, pulled Walter's card out of the corner of the mirror, and dialed.

"Walter Briggs." His voice was professional. Businesslike.

The voice of a person whose life had never been threatened by a psychopath. I was quiet. I almost hung up. Then, after a moment, "Wanda?"

"How'd you know it was me?"

"I heard the television in the background."

"Lots of people watch television."

"I know." He paused, waiting for me to say something. When I didn't, he went on. "Is everything okay?"

"No," I said. "George lost his job."

"George?"

"My ex-husband."

"Ah. The one you want me to sue for not being dead yet?"

"That's the one." I gave a tinny, high-pitched laugh. "Apparently, someone overheard him threatening me on the phone at the refinery office, and he got fired, and he thinks it's my fault. He's on his way to Tennessee to make good on the threat."

Walter's voice tightened. "What was the threat?"

I paused, looked up at the ceiling, trying to remember that last phone call. "Slit my fucking throat, I believe."

Even tighter. "Wanda? Are you okay?"

"Define okay."

"Is he there?"

"No. It's just . . . He wrote me a letter. A crazy fucking psycho letter. When he writes letters, he means it." I put my hand to my forehead and began to babble. "You're the only legal person I know. I have a restraining order, but those are really no good because when someone's crazy, what the hell do they care about a restraining order, right? I mean, if you're going to kill someone, violating a restraining order is like peanuts, right?"

"Wanda. Take a breath."

"I'm okay. I'm okay. Really. I'm fine. I just . . . I'm wondering what I should do. Are you sure we can't sue him for being alive? Because that would make me feel better. You know, make me feel like I'm doing something."

"Wanda. Listen to me. Are you listening?"

I looked around the apartment, trying to focus. "Yeah."

"I want you to pack a bag, quickly, and get over to my house. Do you have a pen and a piece of paper?"

I walked over to the kitchen counter. "Yeah."

He gave me the address. "I want you to meet me there in twenty minutes. Okay? Can you do that?"

"Yeah."

"Twenty minutes. If you're not there, I'm calling the police."

"Twenty minutes," I repeated. I took a deep breath and hung up the phone, then went to my room to pack.

⚬⚬

Walter put the letter on his kitchen counter. I wrapped my fingers around the mug of coffee he'd poured for me. I couldn't drink it—my stomach was too knotted up to allow for that—but the smell held a little comfort.

Walter's house was nice: wood floors, tile in the kitchen, refrigerator with an ice-maker and a water dispenser. Immaculate. Luckily, I was too freaked out to be embarrassed about the state my apartment had been in when he stopped by. Walter was a pipe dream, anyway. Right now I had bigger fish to fry.

"What does this mean? This part about 'I know you remember last time'?" he asked. He was watching me like a hawk, looking for signs of a lie.

"I don't know," I lied. He watched me for a few seconds more, then reached for the phone. I jumped up.

"Whoa, whoa, whoa—what are you doing?"

He paused before hitting the talk button. "I'm calling for pizza, Wanda. What the hell do you think I'm doing? I'm calling the police."

"No!"

He froze, his face tight. "Wanda."

"The cops are not going to help this situation. You're a lawyer. You gonna tell me you don't know what happens when . . ." I trailed off. It didn't matter what Walter knew or didn't know. I'd sent George to jail once. I learned that lesson. I grabbed my bag, battling my shaking hand to keep my grip.

"I'm sorry I called you. I'm gonna go."

Walter put the phone down and stepped toward me. "Where are you gonna go, Wanda? Back home, just wait for him to come and kill you?"

I shrugged. It was a thought. I waved my hand dismissively at him, staring at the natural wood coatrack by the door on which he'd tossed my denim jacket, which looked horribly out of place next to his London Fog raincoat.

Pipe dream.

"This isn't your problem," I said.

He shifted on his feet. "That's bullshit. If you come to me because some maniac is going to kill you, you've just made it my problem."

Walter's anger made my muscles go wooden. I felt George's hands grabbing my arms and leaving bruises. I felt his hot breath on my face. I saw the fury in his eyes as he raised his fist.

Walter touched my arm gently. I screamed and punched him in the chest. Hard. He took a step back and looked at me. I was frozen. I dropped my eyes to avoid seeing the look on his face, but I knew what was there: the same look that had been on the face of everyone who had gotten close to me only to realize that I was so much less than the sum of my parts.

"I'm sorry." I still didn't look at him. I picked up my bag, which had fallen from my grip. "I'm sorry."

His hand was on my arm again. I stopped and looked at it, cursing every tear that fell on it as I crumpled to the floor. He moved slowly down to my side, eventually curling his frame around mine, which was hunched in a fetal position. He smoothed my hair as I cried, and repeated, "Shhhhhhh . . . ," until I regained my breathing.

We stayed there, silent and still, for a long time. Finally, I heard a whisper in my ear. "What did he do to you?"

I was silent. I didn't want to tell him. I didn't want to think about it. I didn't want to move. I just wanted to lie there in the safety of Walter's arms and go to sleep, which was exactly what I did.

When I woke up, it was dark. I was lying on a bed under a flowery quilt, my head resting on a soft pillow tucked inside a clean white pillowcase. A small circular table covered in purple cloth and white lace sat next to the bed, supporting a phone and an alarm clock that read 7:18 p.m. On the wall was a picture of a baby surrounded by sunflowers. Good God. The place looked like Martha Stewart had puked all over it.

I scanned the room, getting my bearings. The closet door was open a bit, and the only thing I could see in it was my duffel bag, slumping in defeat on the floor. I heard a gentle knock, and a tentative shaft of light crept into the room. I looked up and saw Walter leaning against the doorway, keeping his distance, being careful.

"How ya feeling?" he asked. His face was half-lit by the hallway, and his expression was kind, without a hint of pity or condescension. I sighed. Assholes were so much easier to deal with than Jimmy Stewart types.

I pushed myself up to sitting and ran my hand through my hair. "Never better."

He nodded. He had his hands in his trouser pockets, and the top two buttons on his white shirt were undone. I pulled the quilt up around me, covering my torn jeans and Bangles T-shirt. I ran my finger over the purple flower design on the quilt, took a deep breath, and summoned up the courage not to be flippant.

"I'm sorry I hit you."

He held up his hand and shook his head. "Don't worry about it. It's okay."

"It's not okay. I was just freaked out."

"I know."

"You can come in if you want." I gave a feeble laugh. "I probably won't take another swing at you."

He gave a small nod and walked in and sat on the edge of the bed, holding his hand out palm-up. I hesitated, then put my hand in his, feeling the warmth ride up my arm as his fingers closed around mine. I stared out the window and started talking.

ʘ

The first time George hit me, he broke my arm. It wasn't long after we'd moved to Tennessee, and I'd gone to a movie by myself—he'd driven off all my friends by that point—and he was convinced I'd been out with another man. Not long after that, we got married, proving once and for all that I was far stupider than I looked. On our first anniversary, I told him to stop drinking, and he hit me in the face so hard that my right eye was swollen shut for two weeks. I told everyone at work I had been in a car accident. Some of them even believed me. I learned that by smiling and nodding and agreeing to everything that George wanted, I could control the situation. He would still get drunk, call me names, grab me and shake me, but as long as I played the game right, he wouldn't hit. For a long time, I thought I could live that way. I convinced myself it was a life.

George started working for an oil company on the North Slope of Alaska about two years into our marriage. It was a two-weeks-on, two-weeks-off deal; they would fly him back and forth from Anchorage, and my job was to make sure a ticket was waiting there for him to get back to Tennessee. His plan was to move us both up to Anchorage, but I stalled. Every now and again a fight would erupt. He'd want to know why I hadn't quit my job, sold our house and bought one up in Anchorage. I managed to convince him I was trying, and eventually, he would calm down, and then it would be time to drive him back to the airport for his two weeks on.

At first, I stayed in the house and tried to convince myself I missed him when he was gone. I told myself that I looked forward to his daily calls, that I thought it was sweet how he'd grill me on where I'd been if he got the answering machine. A few months into it, I started to venture out. The first place I ventured to was Molly's.

Molly was the traffic manager at Hastings Channel 8. About five years before I met her, her ex, a paralegal named Joel, had stabbed her in the abdomen twelve times. She could smell what was going on with me and George. She gave me books. She told me whom to call. And when I finally packed up and left, she took me in.

For the first six weeks after I left, George went back and forth between the devastated lover who couldn't understand what had happened and the vicious, violent freak who had to control every move I made. It all depended upon the mood and circumstance of the day, and I had no way of knowing whether it would be flowers or dead cats on my doorstep.

Until now, I'd received only one other letter from George, and it was during that time. One afternoon he followed me back to Molly's and cried on the other side of the door, begging me to let him in, to give him one more chance, swearing he didn't mean to hurt me. The next day he slipped a letter under the front door while we were at work. The letter was short; it simply said that he would be back to "cut both you bitches into little pieces." Molly called the police, and they picked George up in a bar two blocks away. He punched the cop and was put in jail; I filed for a restraining order.

Two days later he was out. He bashed down Molly's door and dragged me across the living room by my hair. Molly came down the stairs. Her voice was shaky. She called him Joel. George dropped me on the floor, slamming my head against the wall, and headed over to Molly. He hit her, knocking her down and, as I found out later, breaking her cheekbone. Then he dragged me back to his place, where he kept me trapped with him for three days. He waved a gun in my face, telling me he was going to blow my head off. He burned my things in the fireplace. I still have a scar on my left ankle from the nylon rope he used to bind my legs so I wouldn't run.

On the third day, while I was sleeping, George destroyed what was left of my belongings, then packed up and left. It was another year before the divorce was final.

"Anyway, Molly called a few days after that and told me that she couldn't help me anymore." I reached for the glass of water Walter had gotten for me when my throat started to go dry in the middle of the story. "She never pressed charges against George. I went back to work two weeks later, and she was gone. That was the last time I saw her."

There was a long silence. I guess Walter was waiting to be sure I was done. Finally, he spoke.

"You need to call the police." His tone was low and dead serious. He got up from the bed and grabbed the phone off the night table. Instead of making the call himself, he held it out to me. I stared up at him.

"I think it's something you need to do," he said. His eyes were kind yet firm, so unflinching in the face of the Jerry Springer nightmare he'd just heard. Not too surprising, I guess. The guy was a lawyer. Surely, he'd heard worse. Probably not from anyone sitting in the middle of his regurgitated Martha Stewart guest room, but still . . .

"I'm not ready," I said, not taking the phone from him. I couldn't. The muscles in my arms were shaking. I didn't want him to see that.

"Wanda . . ."

"Walter," I said, "the guy's in Alaska."

Walter shook his head. "Three days ago. If he even sent that letter himself. He might have given it to a friend to put in the mail. He could be anywhere now."

"I need a shower." I didn't know where the hell that came from, but it was as good a change of subject as any. I got up and knelt down by the closet, poking through my bag. No toothbrush. *Crap.* I stood up. Walter was watching me, the phone still clutched in his hand. I sighed.

"Look, Walter, he's lazy. Really, really lazy. He never did a damn thing in his life that required any effort, and coming down to Tennessee from Alaska requires effort. When we were married, if I didn't purchase his ticket for him to get back and forth, he couldn't do it himself. Really. Totally helpless."

Walter's jaw tightened. "How helpless was he when he broke Molly's cheekbone? Or when he put you in the hospital?"

My stomach heaved. I tossed my clean clothes on the bed. "Right, you're right. Fine. But if I'm gonna be killed, I'd rather do it with clean hair. I'd hate to look like crap in all the crime scene photos."

Walter glared at me. An honest-to-goodness glare. Just when I thought I felt about as bad as I could ever feel, I got a glare from Jimmy Stewart. It damn near killed me.

That didn't mean I was going to make anything easy for him, though. Leopards and spots and all that.

I grabbed a sheet of paper from the night table and found a pen inside the drawer. I scribbled a number down and handed the paper to Walter.

"That's his number. Call. If he answers, just hang up and it can wait. If he doesn't, then I'll call the police. Tonight, I promise. But I need to go get my toothbrush."

Walter looked up from the paper in his hand and studied me. "You're not going home," he said finally.

I sighed. "Fine. Where's the closest grocery store?"

⟲

I stood in the express line with a toothbrush and *O, the Oprah Magazine* in my hands, feeling slightly dizzy. The truth was, George could have been anywhere. The truth was, he might have been the laziest son of a bitch alive on an average day, but when he was pissed off, he got very motivated. The truth was, this thing between us probably wasn't over.

The truth sucked.

My exhaustion took over for a minute, and a dizzy spell hit. My balance faltered, bumping me into a guy in front of me. He turned around and helped me steady myself. He was an older guy with a trimmed white beard. Very *Miracle on 34th Street*. He looked kind. And he was wearing a stethoscope.

"Are you a doctor?"

He looked down at the stethoscope, then back at me. He smiled. "So they tell me."

I pointed at his doctor's coat. "I probably should have known by the white coat."

His eyebrows furrowed. "Are you okay?"

"Yeah." I nodded. "I'm pregnant."

What can I say? I'm a big fat liar sometimes. He smiled. "Great, good for you. First child?"

"Yeah." I certainly felt nauseated enough to be pregnant. "Hey, can I ask you a question?"

He smiled. "Shoot."

"If someone is told by a doctor that they're gonna be dead in eight years if they don't quit smoking, and they continue to smoke three packs a day, and ten years goes by . . . shouldn't they be dead already?"

His eyes widened and his smile faltered. "You know, smoking is really bad for the baby."

I shook my head. "Not me. Someone else. I mean, shouldn't he like kick the bucket at any minute?"

The doctor stepped away from me. Must have been an unconscious reflex. "Well, that depends on a variety of factors . . . I really couldn't say." He emptied his basket onto the counter. Three apples and a cup of yogurt. Doctors.

"Look, I'm not going to sue you or anything. I just want to know."

"Miss, I really couldn't . . ." He smiled at the cashier. He looked a little nervous. I have that effect on people sometimes.

I put my hand on his arm. "I'm sorry. I'm not pregnant. It's my ex-husband. He's threatening to kill me and I don't know where he is and I'm so scared that I'm this close to falling over in a dead faint."

The doctor's face softened.

"I mean, three packs a day," I said. "The man should be dead. Shouldn't he be dead?"

He put his hand on mine and gave it a quick pat.

"Absolutely." His eyes were sad. "The end should come any minute now."

Walter was sitting on the sofa when I got back, hands clasped in his lap. He looked tired. The door clicked behind me, and I stood frozen, waiting for him to speak. After a moment, he did, his eyes still on his hands.

"George wasn't there when I called. I know a guy, a private investigator. He's trying to track him down."

There are a number of appropriate responses to someone putting his neck out for you. "Thank you" is one. "Please don't bother, I'll be on my way" is another.

I went with, "Got my toothbrush," waving it lamely in the air.

Walter pushed himself up from the sofa and walked down the hallway. I stood in the foyer, staring at my new toothbrush, wondering if I could run out of the house and pretend none of this had ever happened without seeming insane. I decided I could not.

Shit.

A minute later he returned with a towel. It was white and

fluffy and perfectly folded in thirds. I hoped he had a maid, because any man who folded his towels in thirds was definitely a pipe dream.

But I already knew that about Walter, anyway.

"You decide what you want to do," he said. "I would rather you called the police, but it's your decision, and I'll respect whatever you do. I'm sorry I pressured you about it."

It's amazing, the amount of kindness that can be packed into a small gesture like holding out a towel to someone. I took it from him. He smiled and jerked his head over his shoulder. "The bathroom is the last door on the left."

Again, "Thank you" would have been perfectly appropriate. Me, I came out with, "Don't stare at my ass as I walk away."

He laughed, took me by the shoulders, and turned me around, pointing me down the hallway.

"Go take your shower, Wanda."

I moved on down the hallway, hoping he was watching my ass as I walked, but too chicken to turn around and check.

๑๑

Clean and calm, I walked into the dining room to find a dinner of steak, potatoes, and salad on the table. Walter came out of the kitchen, pulling off an apron and tossing it over the back of a chair.

"Nice spread." I grabbed a baby carrot from the salad and munched it. "But then, it doesn't take much to impress me."

He raised an eyebrow. *Goddammit.* I did it again. I reached over and grabbed his hand.

"I mean, thank you," I said, croaking the words out. "I'm sorry. I have some issues with sincerity."

He smiled that crooked smile. My heart rate kicked up a notch.

"I sensed that," he said. "And you're welcome."

I behaved like a real, live adult through most of dinner. Mom would have been so proud. When we were done, I washed the dishes while Walter polished off his second glass of wine. When I was finished, I folded the kitchen towel—in thirds—and placed it on the counter.

"Dinner was very nice," I said. "Thank you."

"You're welcome." He paused for a moment, watching me. "Are you okay?"

"Yeah. Fine. Why?"

"Well . . ." He paused, looking around the kitchen, then back at me. "You're being so polite."

I crossed my arms. "You're saying I'm not usually polite?"

He staged a sigh. "It's amazing how quickly I can regret saying something with you . . ."

"I'm polite. I'm very fucking polite."

He laughed and held up his hands. "You win. I take it back. I take it all back."

There's a special kind of silence that happens when sexual tension is running the show. It's full of flying glances, flickering smiles, quickening heart rates, and hands occupying themselves by smoothing out sleeves or loosening collars or diving into pockets. If there'd been a third party in the room, they would have wanted to knock us both in the head.

Walter cleared his throat, then disengaged from The Silence by moving past me to wash and dry his wineglass, placing it carefully on the wooden rack before turning back to face me.

"My friend hasn't located your ex-husband, but he called while you were in the shower to tell me that the apartment in Anchorage appears to have been vacated." He looked up, his eyes locked on mine. "That's not a good sign."

I nodded in agreement. He was quiet, watching me. The air around us slowed to a full and complete stop. I couldn't hear a sound but my own breathing.

He reached over and touched my cheek with his fingers, and then with an almost audible crack the air started moving again and the spell was broken. Walter picked up the folded kitchen towel and refolded it, putting it back on the counter before looking at me again.

"Wanda, I think you should stay here. Just until your ex is found. I'm not here much, I won't be bothering you. I just . . ." He sighed and looked around, then back at me and smiled. "To be honest, it's nice having someone here. I think it's a good— temporary—solution for both of us."

I stared at him for a minute.

"Wanda?"

I held up one hand. "I'm thinking."

It occurred to me that I was a horrible decision maker. Look at George. Look at Shooter. Hell, in college I'd been faced with a number of useful majors and chosen liberal arts. I glanced up, and my eyes caught on Walter's. He was wearing the most genuine expression of concern I'd ever seen. Where did this guy come from, anyway? Did he not have problems of his own? What the hell did he want with mine? Was he crazy? He must be crazy. Crazier than me? Not likely. But still . . .

He was obviously just plain nuts.

I sighed, craned my neck, stared down at the little kitchen towel folded in thirds, and before I realized it, I heard the words come out of my mouth.

"Okay. Thank you."

Little crinkles formed at the edges of his eyes. I wanted to touch his face, to express to him how much his help meant to me, to be sincere. Instead . . .

"But if you think you're getting any sex out of this, you've got another think coming, buddy."

He laughed. "You just can't leave a nice moment alone, can you, Wanda?"

I shook my head and gave him my best wiseass grin. He pulled me to him in a gentle hug, his chin resting on the top of my head. I closed my eyes and inhaled, trying to imagine that I could have this, that it wasn't a pipe dream, that pursuing Walter could make sense. It was a big fat lie, but my life was in the shitter and I indulged myself. So sue me.

୧୭

"This is Tony's number, the private investigator looking for your ex. Don't forget to use the peephole before answering the door. This is the code for the security system." Walter rambled on, referencing a list he'd printed out, taking the occasional sip of coffee, which seemed to jog his memory to another detail.

"Avoid going places where George might look for you. Call me if anything happens; my direct line at the office and my cell phone are right here."

In my defense, I did try not to laugh. He took another sip of his coffee and caught my barely suppressed chuckle. "What?"

"Nothing," I said, looking down at the sheet. "You do this on the computer?"

He nodded, and his neck flushed a bit. "I'm sort of a details guy."

I handed him his briefcase. "That's why they pay you the big bucks, Walter."

He gave a sheepish smile and took the briefcase. "Okay. I'll see you tonight, then? Unless you have other plans . . ."

I shook my head and laughed. "My dance card was pretty clear, last time I checked."

He smiled. "Okay." He leaned over, kissed me on the forehead, and left. I watched the door for a while after it had closed, then rubbed my forehead to get the tingling to go away.

I rolled my eyes at myself. Tingling. *Good God.*

I took a quick tour through the house. It was big for a single guy: three bedrooms, a living room, a dining room, kitchen, an office, and a finished basement. All of it immaculate. All of it sterile. I thought about stuffing a pair of my panties into the sofa just for fun but decided against it.

Not on my first day, anyway.

The only sign that anyone actually lived in the place was the mantel in the living room, loaded down with framed pictures. In one of them, a smiling woman who could have been Walter's sister was acting as a human playground for three stair-step kids. In another, an older couple who could have been his parents smiled while dancing at what appeared to be an anniversary party. There wasn't a single picture of Maggie, or of Walter for that matter. Hell, the others could have been the pictures that came with the frames. If the smiling woman hadn't looked so much like Walter, I'd have entertained that possibility.

I went into the guest room and fell back on the bed. I imagined Maggie selecting the quilt I was lying on, carefully straightening the sunflower baby picture until it was perfect. I bet it never occurred to her that someone like me would stay in that room someday.

I sat up and looked around. Maggie was purple flowers and color-coordinated interior design. I was milk crates for bookcases and cheap, do-it-yourself furniture from Wal-Mart. Walter deserved a Maggie. What the hell kind of wiseass God would take her from him and send me instead?

I stood up, suddenly feeling like an intruder in a place I didn't belong. I had to get out. I was a little nervous about leaving, but as long as I didn't return to my apartment or to Hastings Channel 8, I figured I'd be okay. George wouldn't know to look for me anywhere else, and I'd taken Walter's business card with me when I left the apartment, so there was nothing there linking me to him. Besides, George wasn't a connect-the-dots kind of guy. If I wasn't at my apartment when he came to kill me, he'd probably just drink all my booze, pee on my stuff, and be on his way.

Ah. My Prince Charming.

I grabbed my denim jacket off the coatrack and rifled through the pockets for my keys. I needed to be around people who didn't know about George, who wouldn't feel sorry for me, who would give me a healthy dose of shit and make me feel at home again.

I needed Bones.

೦ ೦

"Ow! Dammit, Bones!" I turned around from where I was standing in line for coffee at Osgiliath's, Tennessee's largest used bookstore, to find Joe Bones standing behind me, his cane still raised from giving me a good thump between my shoulder blades. Bones is the oldest, crankiest, and blackest man in Tennessee and the biggest pain-in-the-ass client ever to darken the doors of Hastings Channel 8. Those were just some of the reasons why I loved him.

"What you doing here, girl?" he croaked. Bones croaked everything. "And on a weekday, too. Don't you have a damn job or something?"

I threw him a look and moved up in the coffee line. "I'm between jobs now, Bones."

"You're unemployed is what you are," he said. "I called the station looking for you. They said you got yourself fired. Sheesh."

I grinned, and my tone turned to teasing. "Aw, Bones. You missed me."

"I didn't miss nothin'." He huffed and turned around, thumping the floor with his cane. "I'll be in my office."

The line moved. I watched him stutter his way out of the coffee shop area, taking a left in the bookstore and making for the back. I smiled and stepped up to the counter.

"I want a mocha grande," I said to the kid taking orders. "Bones says it's on the house."

∽

"That Blaine Dowd is a damn fool," Bones grunted when I finished my story about getting fired from Channel 8. No need to tell him any of the stuff after that; the story about Blaine had already gotten him worked up enough. "I've got half a mind to pull all my advertising from that station."

"Yeah, that'll show 'em." I sat back in the comfy chair opposite Bones's desk and sipped my mocha. "When are you gonna give Shelley the big office, Bones? She does all the work around here, anyway."

"I work," he huffed.

"You know, you could go straight to hell for making your granddaughter run the place from the women's bathroom."

"I'm going to hell anyway, so might as well do it from a comfortable office." Shelley had a fine office, just a tad smaller than Bones's, but Bones and I had to maintain a level of antagonism in order to conduct a conversation, and arguing about his office typically did the trick.

Bones raised a wiry white eyebrow at me. "You come here looking for a job?"

"I'm taking some time off."

"You're not gonna work?"

I shrugged. "I came into some money." Between my savings, Dowd's check, and the garnished wages from George's paychecks, I could afford to be a bum for another six months or so. But we both knew that wasn't what Bones was talking about.

He pointed one craggy finger at me. "That's what's wrong with you kids today. I'm eighty-seven years old, and I've never missed a day of work in my life."

I laughed. "Did you just actually say 'you kids today'?"

"You gonna sue that son of a bitch Dowd? You got yourself a good lawyer?"

I shrugged and let a small smile escape. "Maybe."

He raised his other eyebrow. "You're not fucking your lawyer, are you?"

I slapped my hand down on the arms of my chair. "Oh, for Christ's sake, Bones. Can't I just sit and have a cup of coffee in peace?"

He sat back and watched me, his black eyes glittering. "You know Shelley's knocked up again."

"She's married, Bones. Married women don't get knocked up. Women like me get knocked up." I smiled. "Good for her, though. She here?"

He gave a dismissive wave with one craggy hand. "She's over at your old office, trying to get some commercials on with that skittish little blonde."

I nearly spit coffee through my nose. "Are you kidding me?

They put you on Susie's list? Did you make her cry over the phone, or did it take an in-person visit?"

"Don't change the subject. Shelley's going on maternity leave in January, after the holidays."

He looked at me, his thin lips clamped shut. I raised an eyebrow. I knew what he was getting at, but damned if I was going to make it easy on him. Bones and I didn't work that way.

"Again, good for Shelley," I said.

Bones rolled his eyes and leaned forward. "If no one else in town wants you, you can help me manage the place while she's gone, starting the first week of January. It's not good for an able-bodied girl to be lazing around all day like a damn dog."

"You think I'm able-bodied?" I camped up the act of wiping a tear from my eye. "Bones, you're melting my heart."

He shrugged and sat back in his chair with a huff. I took a sip of my coffee.

"Tell you what, Bones," I said finally. "If I'm so desperate for work come January that I won't mind working for the crankiest fucking guy in America, I'll call you."

He chuckled and nodded. I sat back in the chair. It was good to be home.

∽

"Wanda. Yeah, hi. This is Jim McKibbey. I'm a vending machine sales rep. I don't know why you wanted to know, but . . . Well, there you go." *Click.*

I leaned on Walter's kitchen counter, his phone pressed against my face as I retrieved my home messages. There were twelve. One from my landlady, Mrs. Forini, who'd agreed to pick up my mail for me and keep an eye out for anything suspicious. One from Jennifer at the *Hastings Daily Reporter*, notifying me that the charges to my credit card had been reversed, which was good, because the other ten were from nutcases telling me who they were.

"Hi—*giggle, giggle*—Is this, like, one of those radio show things? You know, like on a radio show? Am I on Q94?—*giggle, giggle*—Well, this is Alexandra. Call me!"

Jesus. I half wished the phantom music would visit again. Infuriating as it was, it was better than listening to this. I sighed, tossing the pen I'd been using to take notes across the counter. I punched 7 to delete the message, then moved on to the next one.

"Hi. I'm Elizabeth. I have to say, I'm kind of . . . intrigued why someone would put an ad like that in the paper. I mean, you must be getting a ton of nutcase calls." She laughed. "Hell, you probably think *I'm* a nutcase. Ironically, I'm a therapist. Not that the two are mutually exclusive." Heavy sigh. "This message is going down the shitter fast, isn't it? Well, why not, right? I'm leaving a message with a stranger, and I'm supposed to be the sane one here. Well, fuck it, if you're not selling anything, feel free to give me a call." *Click.*

I stretched over the counter and grabbed the pen, hitting 9 for replay, writing Elizabeth's number down as I heard it the second time. Based on the message, I thought Elizabeth was someone I could talk to. For one, she managed to fit three curse words into less than thirty seconds; I could respect that. Two, she was suspicious I might be selling something, which was exactly what I would think if I saw that crackpot ad. Three, she was a therapist, and while I ordinarily didn't like therapists, who was I to turn down a free headshrink?

And besides, I was so horribly, horribly bored.

I dialed the number, and after four rings, a woman's voice came on the line.

"Hello?"

"Yeah, hi. I'm calling for Elizabeth. Is she in?"

"This is she."

This is *she*. I stood up straighter. "Hi. This is Wanda."

There was a pause. Then a slight intake of breath. Then another pause. "I'm sorry. Wanda?"

"Yes. From the newspaper ad. You called?" I cringed and pressed my palms into my eyes. What was I doing? I used to have friends. I was popular in high school. I *literally* dated the quarterback. How was it possible that I ended up here, with only priests and strange therapists to talk to?

"Oh! Wanda!" She laughed. I relaxed a bit. "The one from the paper?"

"Yeah," I said. "Look, that ad was a mistake."

"Not necessarily," she said, taking a pause. The tone in her voice changed from friendly to oversweet with just a hint of condescension. "I mean, if it helped you to express your feelings . . . I mean, it's important to—"

"No," I said, cutting her off, saving us both the pain. "I mean, it was really a mistake. They screwed it up at the paper. It was meant for this other person, and . . . It doesn't matter."

I heard some breath release from the other end. "Crap. I'm sorry. I didn't mean to sound like I was lecturing." She sighed again, and then a quiet self-admonition: "I always do that."

"Hmm? Do what?"

"Talk down to people. I hate it, but I can't help it. They start talking, and then there's a pause, and I'm supposed to jump in and be brilliant, but usually what I'm thinking is that I wish they would stop all the whining, and so I go into this college textbook crap." She gave a frustrated sigh. "It's awful."

"Maybe you need to find a new line of work."

"Yeah, if you can think of one that allows me to be here when the kids come home from school, I'm open. I've got some clients who would thank you, I'm sure." She laughed. It was a genuine, hearty laugh. I liked it.

"Well, you're gonna hate this. Part of the reason I called is because I have something I kind of need to talk about."

"Oh," she said. Her sunshine voice came back. "Sure, Wanda, that's great. Go ahead."

"Um . . . how about this? I tell you what I'm thinking about, and you try to stay out of Pollyanna land, okay? You can be my practice therapist, and I can be your practice client. You tell me if I'm crazy, and I tell you if you're weird. What do you think?"

"We don't like the term *crazy*," she began.

"Weird," I warned.

"Is that why all my clients keep leaving me?"

"I'd take that bet, yes."

"Well, shit." She laughed again, and her voice went natural. "Go ahead. What's your problem?"

"It's kind of a moral question. I was just watching the news, and they had this story about this crabbing boat in Alaska."

"The one that went down and all the crew members died?" Chopping in the background. Sounded like a good idea. I opened the fridge and started to poke around.

"Yeah. Well, my ex-husband is in Alaska and he just lost his job and I know those crabbers always need people and I'm actually sitting here praying that he was on that boat." The chopping in the background stopped. I visualized Elizabeth taking an unconscious step back. I grabbed a bag of baby carrots and shut the door to the fridge. "That makes me a bad person, doesn't it?"

A moment of silence. The chopping resumed. "I can't do this."

"Why?"

"Because there's a huge difference between what I'm supposed to tell you and what I want to tell you."

"What's the difference?"

"Okay. What I'm supposed to tell you is that there's no value to defining something as 'good' or 'bad.' Then I'm supposed to ask you how those thoughts made you feel."

"Good fucking God."

"No shit," she said, her voice laced with a combination of frustration and mild amusement. "Fifty thousand dollars on my education and this is what I'm telling people."

I slouched over the kitchen counter and grabbed a handful of nuts from a wooden bowl Walter had set out. "So what was the other thing?"

"Hmm?" she said.

"What you were really thinking. What was it? That I'm evil, right?"

"No," she said, dismissing the idea with a huff. "Look, thinking bad thoughts is human. Everyone does it. It's only a problem if you act on those thoughts. So unless you secured your ex a position on a boat you knew was going to sink, you need to just get over yourself and start spending your energy on things that matter."

Whoa. I stopped slouching against the counter. "Really?"

Elizabeth sighed. "Yes, really."

I smiled. I could get used to this chick. "If it's any comfort, I liked your second answer better."

The food prep sounds ceased in the background. "You did?" she said.

"Yeah. Deliver smackdown next time. Works for Dr. Phil."

She laughed. "Yeah, well, Dr. Phil's not a single mom with a lawsuit hanging over her head." There was a kid's voice in the background. Elizabeth said something, and I could hear her give the kid a kiss.

"So what about phantom music?"

"I'm sorry?" she said. I sighed. She didn't like the term *crazy*, but I was pretty sure *nuts* would be making an appearance soon.

"I've been hearing phantom strands of music. Mostly at night, when I'm going to sleep. No one else can hear it. Am I crazy?"

Pause. *Yes.* "Not necessarily. It's probably just your subconscious talking."

"Okay. Weird."

"No, I'm serious."

"But it started after a head injury," I said. "Don't you think that's something of a coincidence?"

"Well, either life is full of coincidences, or there's no such thing as coincidence," she said.

"Weird."

She huffed. "I was serious that time, too."

I let that go. "Okay, but why would my subconscious wait until I got knocked in the head to speak up?"

She grunted. "Beats the shit out of me. It's your subconscious."

"Yeah. Okay." Moving on. "What was that about a lawsuit?"

"Oh, Christ," she said, lowering her voice. "How much time do you have?"

෮෯

"What kind of lawyer are you again?"

Walter had just put his coat on the rack and was loosening his tie when I bounded out of the kitchen, sliding a bit in my socks on the hardwood floors and wiping my hands on my Billy Joel Storm Front tour T-shirt.

"Civil." He put his briefcase down and looked over my shoulder. "What's that smell?"

I glanced behind me at the kitchen door. "The reason I ordered pizza tonight."

He raised an eyebrow at me. "What did you do?"

"Me?" I gave an innocent shrug. "Nothing. It's my friend Elizabeth who needs a lawyer. Oh—did you mean in the kitchen?"

He stepped back and eyed me. "Have you been drinking?"

"No. I saw this recipe on the Food Network for this chicken-with-leeks dish and you didn't have leeks, you had scallions, and I didn't really know the difference, but . . . Well, it wasn't pretty. But it's all clean. I'm just running the fan to clear the smoke."

Walter laughed and put both hands on my shoulders. "Take a breath, Wanda."

I inhaled. "I'm fine. Really. It's just being in the house alone all afternoon and thinking about George . . . I've just got some nervous energy I need to burn off."

There was a beat when the idea of burning off energy floated between us. Walter pulled his hands away from my shoulders. I stepped back. Jesus. We were worse than kids passing notes in study hall. *Do you like me? Or do you* like *like me?*

"So what's going on with your friend?"

"She took her ex-husband's car and drove it over his rototiller. The bastard deserved it—they were trying to reconcile, and she caught him sleeping with a bimbo from Hastings Flowers—but now he's suing her for the damage to the car and the value of the rototiller. I gave her your direct number. I hope that's okay."

He laughed. "Yeah, that's fine." There was a long silence, then a conversational downshift. "Have you heard anything? About your ex-husband?"

I shook my head. "No news is good news, right?"

He shrugged, paused. "Have you called the police?"

I felt my shoulders tighten. "No."

He took off his suit jacket and placed it over the back of a chair. I shifted on my feet.

"Walter, you just don't understand."

He turned to face me. "Explain it to me, then."

"Calling the police is not going to help the situation."

"What harm can it do?"

"Maybe you should ask Molly that question."

His face hardened. I felt regret snake its way through my gut, but I kept my eyes steely on his, refused to show any signs of softening. In for a penny, in for a pound.

He looked away first.

"Excuse me," he said, his eyes avoiding mine as he walked past me, down the hall to his room. I turned and watched him go, letting out a breath as the door shut gently behind him.

"Dammit," I whispered, my eyes unconsciously floating toward the mantel in the living room, where there wasn't a single picture of his dead wife. My eyes shut tight as it occurred to me for the first time that maybe, just maybe, Walter's trying to protect me didn't have as much to do with me as I might think.

Crap. I shouldn't be here. I should be taking Edgar Dowd's ten grand and blowing it in Vegas. Or drinking mai tais in Maui. Something, anything, as long as it didn't involve dragging other people into my drama. *I* didn't even want to be involved in my drama. I turned around to go back to my room and pack, but Walter was standing behind me, blocking my way.

We stared at each other for a moment of excruciating silence. He'd traded his office clothes for a pair of jeans and a sweatshirt that read "Harvard Law School." I stared at his chest as he spoke.

"You're right. I don't know what you're going through." He ran his fingers through his hair. I kept my eyes focused on the "Har" in "Harvard." "I just don't want to see you get hurt."

I nodded, motioning to his chest. "You went to Harvard?"

He looked down at the shirt, then back at me. "Yeah."

That moment ranks number one on my list of the Stupidest Things That Have Ever Made Me Want to Cry. Who cared that he went to Harvard? Who cared that he was trying to save me because he couldn't save her? Who cared that I would never be good enough for him, no matter how hard I tried, no matter how much I changed, if I even could change?

I did. Goddammit, I cared. And there I stood, the incurable wiseass, rendered mute by a stupid freaking sweatshirt.

Walter reached out, pulling me slowly to him. His body smelled earthy and fragrant, one part Irish Spring and two parts pure man, and for the second time in five minutes, I had to swallow a lump in my throat. I tightened my grip around his waist, buried my face in his chest, inhaled deeply, and forced myself to be sincere.

"I'm sorry," I choked out. "I totally suck at letting people help me."

He pulled back a bit, his palms resting gently on either side of my neck, his thumbs tracing my jawline. My heart worked double time, pounding out what I believe was Morse code for *Kiss me.*

"Wanda." His whisper was ragged, questioning. Here he was, mine for the taking—all I had to do was lean in and let fly—and instead, I gasped and pushed myself out of his arms.

"You know what?" I said, my words stumbling over each other to get out. "The pizza's gonna be here in a minute and I need to get my cash. Don't argue. It's on me. I'll be right back."

I ran down the hallway into the Martha Stewart guest room and shut the door behind me, putting my hands over my eyes and leaning against the door, my chest heaving as I gasped for air, my heart pounding out its futile message in Morse code: *Kiss me, kiss me, kiss me.*

Too bad no one was listening.

The pizza's gonna be here?" Elizabeth asked, incredulous. "He was going to kiss you and you said, 'The pizza's gonna be here'?"

"I know." I dropped my head into my hands, staring down at my burger and fries. "There just aren't enough *o*'s in the word *smooth* for me, are there?"

"So what happened after that?"

"We ate dinner and went to bed." Her eyes widened and I held up my hand to ward off any bright ideas. "Separately."

She nodded, watched me for a minute, then spoke again. "He's taking my case, you know."

"Really?" Even though I'd referred her, I felt a stab of stupid jealousy. Elizabeth, as fate would have it, was thin, blonde, and naturally beautiful. It took every last bit of self-esteem I had not to hate her on sight. "You saw him?"

She nodded and poked at her salad. "This morning. He's really cute."

"You're not helping," I groaned, putting my face in my hands.

"Not trying to," she said, grinning. "I think glasses are sexy on a guy. Don't you?"

"Shut up," I said. "He's just a nice guy, trying to help a pathetic case of a woman, that's all."

She rolled her eyes. "Oh, please. I saw it in his eyes when I mentioned your name, and your face shouts it out like a damn billboard. You guys are a hairsbreadth away from the big bang. Better accept it now, or you'll be taken by surprise with your legs all hairy."

I raised one eyebrow. "The big bang?"

"Denial . . . ," she sang as she poked at a cherry tomato.

I slammed my palm down on the table. "What are you doing eating a salad? If you turned sideways in the wind, you'd whistle."

Elizabeth took a sip of her water. "You know, it's just as rude to make fun of a skinny person as it is a fat person. And don't change the subject. We're talking about *your* screwed-up life, not mine."

"You're gonna need to start taking some of this hostility out on real clients soon, or I'm gonna start charging you."

"Ooh, nice deflection, but we're still talking about you and Walter. Now, tell me. Why is it so bad that you've got a thing for him? It's obvious the feeling's mutual."

I ticked off my points on the fingers of one hand. "(A)It's not obvious. (B) He went to Harvard. (C) He's a lawyer. (D) He folds his towels in thirds."

She raised her eyebrows. "Really?"

"See what I mean?" I said. "We're not compatible. He's a fine French Merlot, and I'm that crappy blush that comes in a box."

Elizabeth was quiet. I looked up. "What?"

"Blush in a box?" she said. "I think that's the worst piece of shit analogy I've ever heard. And I'm a therapist."

"Whatever." I tossed down the french fry I'd been dangling over my plate. "My point is—"

"Your point is that you think you're not good enough for him." She sat back and crossed her arms over her stomach. "I cannot believe your arrogance."

"Arrogance?" I sputtered. "What the—?"

She pointed her finger at me. I shut up. "You don't even know this guy, and you think you know what he needs? Who died and left you to decide what is and is not right for him? If he wants to be with you, and you want to be with him, and you're not letting it happen because of blush in a box, then go ahead and run away now and save him the misery of loving you. I have a mother-in-law apartment over my garage if you want it."

She sat back and smiled. "That felt good. I'm going to start doing that with clients. Today." She winked at me. "Thanks, Wanda."

"I'm glad to be of service," I said, my voice in full pout.

"Oh, stop being hurt," she said. "You'll thank me later. It's common sense. Either fix the problem or get out before you make everyone crazy."

She reached for her water. I stared at a piece of wilted lettuce hanging out of my burger. "So how do I do that?"

"Hmm?" she said. "Do what?"

I huffed. "Don't you pay attention to your own stupid advice? How do I fix it?"

"Well, you can get over this blush-in-a-box crap, to start with." She reached over to my plate, grabbed a fry, and popped it into her mouth. "You know, you're right about the salad. I'm getting a burger next time."

⤲

I returned to Walter's place with an emotional hangover and a package of yellow sticky notes. Elizabeth had given them to me, explaining that I was to write on them specific things I wanted and stick them on my wall, pulling each one down as I achieved the goal. She said the exercise was her idea, something she had done after she caught her husband, Jack, in bed with the girl from Hastings Flowers.

"Made me feel better," she said. "And it kept me from killing him. Everybody plays, everybody wins."

I lay back on the bed and flipped the package of sticky notes over and over in my hands, having no idea what to write on them. What did I want? Did I want to be a kinder, gentler Wanda? Did I want Walter? Did I want a job? Did I want to find George dead on the side of the road? And how the hell were sticky notes supposed to help me with any of that? I wasn't going to say anything to Elizabeth, because she was the first real friend potential I'd had in a long while, but resolving problems with sticky notes seemed like the stupidest thing I'd ever heard of.

I sighed and picked up the phone, dialing my home number to check my messages.

There was only one. It was from George.

"Wanda." I could barely make out the voice in the static on the line, but knew who it was. Ice shot through my veins, and I almost dropped the phone as I made out what I could of the rest of the message. "I'm in—*static*—Kansas. I need to talk to you. You have to—*static*—listen to me—*static*—Call me at—*static*—4-5—*static*—7-3-9."

I sat motionless as my answering machine requested I save, forward, or delete the message. Eventually, the machine hung up on me. I realized my breathing was shallow, and I inhaled deep.

Crap. Why the hell was I cowering in hiding from this guy? Why didn't I just get a gun, go to my own apartment, and let nature take its course?

Well, there were a lot of reasons. I didn't want to kill anyone. I didn't want to die.

And the other reason was due home in about an hour.

I dropped the phone to the floor and curled up under the covers, pulling them over my head, the way I did when I was little and was convinced the monsters in my closet would eat me alive if not for the amazing protective powers of bed linens.

〇〇

I woke up to the sound of my door creaking. I pulled the covers down to see Walter standing in the shaft of light at my doorway. His tie was loose, his top shirt buttons were open, and his hair was rumpled on one side as though he'd been resting his head on his hand for a while.

"Hey," I said, pushing myself up to a sitting position. "What time is it?"

"Nine," he said softly. "I didn't mean to wake you, but you've been passed out for a while. I thought you might be hungry."

I shook my head. "I had a big lunch."

He nodded. "Okay." He smiled and started to shut the door behind him, then opened it up again. "I've been working on a case all night, and I need a break. You in the mood for some wine?"

"For a while," Walter said, stretching his legs over his cream-colored leather sofa, "I thought it would get better. That it would be easier to come home and see the pictures, her things. They say it takes about a year. They lie."

An empty bottle of wine sat on the coffee table next to a ceramic bowl filled with grapes. The fire rolled gently in the fireplace. I couldn't see the clock, but I imagined it to be somewhere near midnight.

"One day I packed all her stuff up in a rental truck and hauled it down to storage. I haven't been there since." He took a sip of his wine and then gestured with his glass toward the pictures on the mantel. "Those are mostly of my sister and her kids."

I nodded, trying to think of an appropriate comment, something that showed my sensitive side. I drew a big fat blank.

Walter looked up on my silence and smiled. My heart lurched in my chest at the sight of him in the firelight, loose tie and rolled-up sleeves giving him that sexy disheveled look. Damn Elizabeth and her damn self-awareness. Let's talk about your *feelings*, Wanda. *Pffft.* I took a sip of wine.

"Let's move on to something more interesting than my sob story," he said, bringing me back into the moment. He popped a grape into his mouth and chewed thoughtfully for a few moments. "Let's talk about that day in your apartment."

"Hmmm?" I said, wincing as a few drops of wine cut through my throat. I choked briefly, then looked up at Walter through misty eyes.

"You okay?" he asked.

"Yeah," I croaked. "Wrong pipe."

"Ahhh." He looked down at his glass, then back at me. "If you don't want to talk about it, then . . ."

"No," I said, recovering. "We can talk about it. I'm just not sure what there is to say."

His eyes flickered at me. "You're not?"

"No. I mean, I kissed you, and then I thought we were going to have sex, but you kinda freaked out, and then I grabbed your crotch, and you screamed like a girl—"

"I *know* what happened," he said, holding up a hand to shut me up. "Any chance we can wipe that 'screamed like a girl' thing off the record?"

I smiled and shook my head. "I don't think so."

"Fine. Look, we both know what happened. What I want to talk about is . . ." He paused, huffed a short laugh at whatever was going through his mind, and stared into the fire as he went on. "I just think we should talk about *why* it happened."

"You wanna talk about why?"

He met my eye. He was dead serious. "Yeah. Why did you kiss me?"

My throat tightened, and my breathing kicked up a notch. "I don't know. I thought you were cute, I'd had a few drinks . . ."

"I see," he said with a brief nod.

"Dammit," I said. "I didn't mean that it was just because I'd been drinking. I meant . . . Ugh!" I slammed my fist down on the sofa cushions. "Why are you asking me this?"

He sat forward, put both of our glasses on the coffee table, and took my hands in his. My entire body buzzed at his touch, and my jury was out on whether I was going to jump him or run screaming from the room.

"I think it's time we talked about it." He brought his eyes up to meet mine and smiled his crooked smile. Made of kryptonite, that smile. "I think there's a thing going on here between us. I just want to make sure it's mutual before . . ."

"Before . . . ?" I knew what he was going to say, but I had to draw it out. It had to be on paper before I'd believe it.

He held my gaze. "Before I act on it."

I dropped my eyes, felt my cheeks blazing. "So you think we've got a thing?"

He let go of my hands. "You don't?"

I shook my head and lied through my stupid lying teeth. "No."

He looked at me, reading me. He had to know I was lying.

Please, Walter, I thought, *can't you just save us both the pain and see through me?*

He stood up, picking up our wineglasses. "Okay. My mistake, then."

I watched him retreat to the kitchen and listened as he washed the glasses. I stood up and backed away from the sofa, as though my total mess of a life was all the fault of cream-colored leather. I stopped when the frigid window shocked my back, and I froze against it, grateful for the harsh reality of the chilling cold.

Walter returned a minute later and leaned against the wall on the opposite side of the living room from me. He looked good, backlit by the light coming through the kitchen door, a small white towel draped over his shoulder. My breathing went shallow.

He wanted me. He'd put it on paper. And yet there I was, pressing my back against a freezing-cold window, trying to fend off the one thing I really wanted. It's a good thing I'd been getting chummy with a therapist. I'd never be able to afford all the help I needed if I had to pay for it.

He gave a small smile and I felt a rush. He was seeing through me, doing all the work for me. "Is there something you want to talk about?"

I shook my head. "No."

He took a step forward. "You seem a little . . . disturbed."

"That's not unusual for me."

He continued moving toward me, tossing the kitchen towel on the coffee table as he passed. I pushed my back into the glass. A moment later he was standing so close that I could inhale the sweet wine on his breath.

"What's disturbing you?" he asked.

"I don't know."

He leaned one hand against the window, then pulled it back quickly.

"Jesus, that's cold." He put his hands on my shoulders and guided me back to the sofa. He sat next to me, one leg curled toward me, one arm casually draped over the back, his fingers lightly grazing my shoulder and sending snapping currents of electricity down my spine.

"You're shivering," he said.

"The window. It was cold." I stiffened as his hand moved from the sofa to rub my shoulder.

"You okay?" he asked, backing away a little.

"Yes," I said. "I mean, no."

"Wanda, what's going on here?"

I closed my eyes and let the wine speak.

"I'm afraid you're going to kiss me." *Oh. God. Take me now. A lightning bolt would be great, but an aneurysm will do.*

"And would that be a bad thing?" he asked.

I opened my eyes and let out a stuttering breath. "No."

He smiled. "Are you sure?"

"No," I said.

He laughed and reached to push a strand of hair away from my eyes. "You are so . . . strange."

"Well, there's some sweet talk for you." I gave one of those high-pitched, self-conscious laughs and put my head in my hands. Walter's hand slid down to my back. I jumped up off the sofa, still hiding my face.

"Wanda?" I heard him get up, felt him take my arms, pulling my hands away from my face. One finger hooked under my chin and lifted it. Our eyes met. My blood was pumping, my breathing erratic. I focused on his eyes, running down my face, over my chin, landing on my lips. "I can't figure you out."

"Hang on," I said. "I've got a manual in the trunk of my car."

He laughed. "I might need that. You practically jump me in your apartment, and now . . ." He traced one finger down the side of my face. *Hoo-wah.* "I guess I just don't understand."

"Well," I stammered, "back then, we hardly knew each other. And now . . ."

I couldn't finish the sentence. He leaned in closer. "And now what?"

I looked away, trying to concentrate on my feet rather than Walter's breath fluttering against my cheek. "And now I know you."

"Ah," he said. "Well, that makes sense."

I shrugged. "Does to me."

He nodded, more serious. "Could you pretend I'm a stranger, then? Because if I don't kiss you soon, I'm going to have to leave the room."

"Do you always announce when you're going to kiss someone?" I asked, trying to be funny, but my delivery was thrown off by my shortness of breath.

He shook his head. "No."

He put his hand in my hair, running his fingers through it and making my body surge with heat. I leaned my face into the warmth of his palm, and he moved closer, his cheek almost touching mine, his breathing rough against my ear.

"I'm going to explode if you don't say it's okay for me to kiss you soon," he said, his voice quiet and raw.

"It's okay," I whispered. The words were barely out before his arm snaked around my waist. His lips were soft at first, becoming gradually more insistent as we rode the first wave and surfed it. His eyes were on soft focus when we finally pulled apart.

"Are you okay?" he asked.

My heart was banging around in my chest like a freaked-out parakeet. I gave up the fight. I was a goner. There was no way around it now.

"No," I said. His face tightened, and he moved away, but I grabbed his tie and pulled him back to me to surf another wave. He tasted fresh and clean, like grapes. He pulled me in tighter this time, mashing our bodies together, his arms and his tongue grappling over me like this was his only chance. My eyes were still closed when he finally pulled away, and it took a moment for me to focus on him and see that he was smiling.

"I won't scream like a girl this time," he said, his grin exuberant and boyish, his cheeks flushed.

I laughed, locking my hands behind his neck and leaning my forehead to his, looking up into his eyes, thoughts of blush in a box taking a backseat to the rush of happiness I was finally allowing myself to feel.

"You know," I said, "it's been three years since I've done this."

"That's okay," he said with a grin. "I hear it's like riding a bike."

"No, what I'm saying is, it's been *three years*." I accentuated the last words by tugging on his tie in two short jerks. He laughed and put his hand on my face.

"You're incredible," he said.

"Tick-tock, Romeo," I said. "I've got some lost time to make up for."

The first time, it was like we were starving, all nibbling and biting and rushing toward the finish. The second time, it was slower, rhythmic, deliberate. We didn't bump into the coffee table once that time. The third time was more exploratory, less explosive, and afterward we fell into a mingled clump on the floor, catching our breath and grazing our fingers over each other.

After a while, Walter got up to nudge the fire back into a full blaze. He pulled the blanket off the sofa, spooning his naked body behind mine on the rug, snuggling his face into the back of my neck.

"That was fun," he said, his words running together as his breath started to even out.

"Mmmm-hmmm," I said, my eyes half-closed.

"I love you," he whispered, and his breathing tapered into a light snore. My eyes flew open.

I knew he hadn't meant it. He couldn't have meant it. It was probably just something he said. Maybe it was a residual habit from when Maggie was alive, and he was just too tired to realize he'd said it to me.

But *I* realized it. I watched the fire and tried to reason the tears away, but they kept coming, anyway. Had he not said it, I might have stayed. But the severity of the stab that came from hearing those words, murmured in a sleep-driven exhale, was an indication that it was way past time to get out. There were other places where I could hide from George. If I stayed with Walter, I'd be gambling more than I could afford to lose.

I crawled out from under his arms, and he rolled over onto his back but didn't wake up. Once I was dressed, I pulled the blanket up to cover his chest. I kneeled over him and kissed him lightly, giving him one last chance to wake up and pull me back. He didn't. I watched him sleep for a little while and then went to my room to gather my things. I put his key on the kitchen counter and closed the door behind me. I sobbed quietly as I walked to my car, then got behind the wheel and lost six hours driving through the winding roads of Hastings.

At nine that morning, my eyes red and my heart tired, I showed up at Elizabeth's doorstep. Without a word, she led me to the small apartment above her garage, and I fell onto the bed and slept for the next twelve hours.

෴

The knocking woke me up. I glanced at the clock on the wall: 9:17.

"Come in," I mumbled in a hoarse whisper. A second later Elizabeth was sitting on the edge of my bed holding out a mug of hot chocolate.

"With marshmallows," she said. I sat up and took the mug, sipping quietly, my mind still emerging from the fog.

"You wanna talk about it?" she asked after a few minutes. "I'm a *great* fucking shrink."

I smiled and shook my head. "I just think it's best that I get out now, you know, before it goes too far."

She nodded. "Went too far, huh?"

I mustered up a cynical laugh and said, "Yep."

She took a sip of her cocoa, and her eyes traveled the small room in a quick sweep. "Sorry about this place. My ex–mother-in-law designed it. Yellow walls." She shuddered. "Igh."

I hadn't given the room more than a glance when I came in. It was large and open, with one door leading out to the landing and stairs and another door leading to the bathroom. The bed was a double, sitting in the corner. The floor was hardwood, with a large woven rug covering the middle. There was a desk under the window, a dresser in the opposite corner from the bed, and a freestanding wardrobe. Everything a girl hiding from her psycho ex-husband needed.

"I like it," I said finally. "How much is the rent?"

Elizabeth shrugged. "Nothing, unless you decide you want to stay for good. We can take it day by day."

I smiled. "Thanks."

She patted my leg and got up, putting a set of keys on the desk. "You can share the kitchen and living room with us. Come on down anytime. The kids are excited to meet you tomorrow."

I nodded. Elizabeth disappeared, the sound of her footsteps getting lighter and lighter as she made her way down. I fell back on the bed, watching the lights from passing cars swish across the ceiling until I fell asleep again.

I stayed in the apartment for three days, coming out only to run to the store for bottled water and oranges, which was pretty much what I lived on. I didn't want to see or talk to anyone. Elizabeth seemed to sense this, and she left me alone.

I found a notebook and a pen in the desk drawer, and I wrote furiously in it. I wrote about how every Christmas my father and I would stay up late and watch *The Philadelphia Story* together. I wrote about my mother and me trying to sew a costume for Halloween when I was twelve and failing miserably. I wrote about Miss Maria's School of Dance, remembering how Miss Maria—who was actually a Hungarian refugee named Magda—would cup my chin in her rough hands and say in her thick voice, "Nevah have I seen a child so happy as dees vun."

She was right. I had been a happy kid. No reason not to be. My parents had a good marriage. I was an only child. I got everything I needed, and Dad taught me the value of working for the extras, like designer jeans and boom boxes. I'd had every advantage. So how had I ended up here? How had I gone from the graceful little girl doing pirouettes for Miss Maria to the graceless tumbling witness in Pencil Face's School of Crappy Cross-Examination?

Beat the hell out of me. My teachers seemed to think I had a great life in the bag, based on how they nagged me all through high school. *You have so much potential, Wanda. What are you going to be when you grow up, Wanda? A smart kid like you can do whatever she wants, Wanda.*

Only I didn't know what I wanted to do. I was good in science and math. Fair to middlin' in social studies. Excelled in English. And yet, for all that, I never knew what I really wanted. I still didn't know. So why were all those people always cheering me on, sure I would master whatever I set my mind to do? I asked my English teacher Mrs. Knickie that question when I beat out Annie McGee, the valedictorian, for Most Likely to Succeed.

"You're a go-getter," she'd told me with a wink. "We'll all be watching you for great things."

Great things. Yeah. I'd pissed my twenties away on a bad marriage and was starting my thirty-second year hearing phantom strands of a song I couldn't identify while hiding from an ex who wanted to kill me. I wonder what Mrs. Knickie would have to say if she could see me now? Would she be able to adequately express her disappointment using ten words from the SAT vocabulary list?

It occurred to me, during this furious journaling, that there were two ways to look at it. One, everyone had been wrong and I was just a loser from day one. Two, I'd actually been so afraid to fail that I deliberately threw my life in the toilet and kept flushing until every last remnant of who I had been was washed away.

Ding ding ding. Thanks for playing. We have a winner.

Welcome to Self-Fulfilling Prophecies 101, I wrote in the notebook. *My name is Wanda Lane, and I would have a syllabus for you if only I had bothered to actually create one. Don't be disappointed, though; it would have sucked, anyway.*

My handwriting at this point was scratchy, and my hand ached, but I pushed through until the next sentence was done.

I am the stupidest human being on the planet.

With that, I tossed the notebook to the floor and grabbed my toothbrush and a towel from the wardrobe.

§

I had just gotten out of the shower when Elizabeth knocked at my door. I was still amped up from my journey of self-discovery, and I opened the door quickly, then continued flying around the room, organizing the pens, smoothing the bedspread. Elizabeth seemed surprised and stepped into the room cautiously as I pulled the towel off my head and scrubbed it over my hair.

"I was going to come up here and yell at you to get your sorry ass together," she said. "Looks like my work here is already done."

She plopped on the bed, and I pulled the chair over from the desk, rubbing my face and tossing the towel onto a pile of laundry on the floor.

"Yeah, sorry about that. I just needed some time to get my head together. But I think I'm better now. I think I've hit on what I've been doing wrong, which is pretty much everything." I rambled at the speed of light. She crossed her legs and stared me down.

"Then I guess you'll be okay if I talk to you about Walter?" she asked.

I froze at the sound of his name. Although I had been thinking about him, weaving him into my hopeful vision of the future as I examined my past, the sound of his name cut a swath through my gut, and I deflated a little.

"I saw him today," she said. "He's worried about you."

I looked at her. "Did you tell him I was here?" My throat tightened just talking about Walter.

Elizabeth shook her head. "No. I told him I'd talked to you and that you were okay."

"Thanks," I said softly. I lay back across the bed, my feet tapping nervously on the floor. We both stared at the ceiling.

"You gonna tell me what happened with you two?" she asked.

"Not now," I said, still staring. "I have too much to do."

"Like what?" she asked.

I turned to face her. "You got any more of those sticky notes?"

Elizabeth nodded and excused herself, returning five minutes later with two Diet Cokes, some markers, and two packages of sticky notes. She pulled one marker cap off using her teeth and let out a garbled "Let's get cracking."

"What do I do?"

She scribbled on a sticky note and held it up for me. It said "Get a job." She spit the pen cap onto the floor and pulled the note off the pad, slapping it on my wall.

"A reinvention of self is half commonsense planning and half blindly following out-of-nowhere hunches," she said. "First, we do free form. Just write anything that comes to mind that you might want to improve about yourself."

"I don't have that kind of time," I said.

"Let me finish. Then, when you're done, evaluate what you've written. You'll see some patterns develop. Then you whittle it down to about ten things you really need to do. You do them and boom—you're a brand-spankin'-new Wanda."

I stared at her. "And this worked for you?"

She shrugged. "I'm a work in progress. Get writing, girl."

It was after eleven when we stopped, sitting Indian-style on the floor, surrounded by scrunched-up notes, staring at a wall speckled with square, sticky, yellow directives that were supposedly going to change my life.

"Am I crazy for wanting to do this?" I asked.

"We don't like the term *crazy*," she said.

I grabbed a pillow and threw it at her. We were quiet for a moment, then Elizabeth spoke up again. "I wish you wouldn't wait to talk to Walter. He's really worried about you, you know."

"Can't. Gotta go one step at a time. If he doesn't want me when I'm done, then I'll have to live with that. But if he takes me back now, I'll never do this. And I need to do this."

I sat forward and looked at her. She was staring at the wall of sticky notes. "Promise me you won't say anything to him. Just that I'm okay and he shouldn't worry. Please, Elizabeth."

"Okay. You've got my word." She sighed. "So what are you going to do first?"

"I don't know," I said, my eyes grazing over the wall of tasks. "It's kind of overwhelming. Maybe you should pick one at random for me?"

"Sure." She pulled herself onto the bed, covered her eyes, and grabbed a sticky note off the wall. I stood up and took it from her.

"This one should be easy," I said, laughing and showing it to her. She cocked her head to read it at an angle.

"Get a job," she read. "Looks like you've got a big day tomorrow."

I smiled. "Looks like."

She got up and gave me a hug. "Blueberry pancakes. Six-thirty. You're not there, I'm coming in after your ass, and I promise it won't be pretty."

7

Kids, this is Wanda. She's going to be staying in the apartment over the garage for a while."

I nodded at the children and gave a grunt to the effect of "Good morning." I'm not a big morning person.

Elizabeth put the pancakes on the table, and the kids descended on them like vultures. Alex was a hair-in-the-eyes teenager; I'd place him at about fifteen. Based on his T-shirt, jacket, and backpack, he had something of a Nike obsession. He seemed the quiet, contemplative type. Kacey, a pixieish preteen with brown hair and the brightest blue eyes I'd ever seen, looked to be about twelve. She was not so quiet.

"I like Avril Lavigne and Justin Timberlake. Do you like Justin Timberlake?" she asked. Elizabeth put a cup of coffee in front of me, God bless her.

"Leave Wanda alone, Kace," she said, sitting down next to me. "She's not used to being up this early in the morning."

"Even if I did like Justin Timberlake, I wouldn't admit to

it," I said, reviving slowly as the caffeine blasted the sleep out of my veins.

"What's Wham!?" she asked. I looked down at my T-shirt, where George Michael and Andrew Ridgeley gave cracked, ironed-on smiles.

I lifted my coffee and took another sip. "You're better off not knowing."

"The blond one's kinda cute," she said with a shrug. I gave her points for generosity.

Elizabeth waved her hands at the kids. "Hurry up; eat. You'll miss the bus, and I don't have time to take you in."

The kids inhaled their breakfasts and gave their mother swift kisses before heading out the door. I watched them go, then leaned over to Elizabeth.

"Did I just see a soldering iron hanging out of Kacey's backpack?" I asked.

Elizabeth smiled. "She's doing some kind of presentation at school. Kacey's an engineering wunderkind. To date, she's fixed the VCR, the clock on the coffeemaker, and my electric toothbrush. My biggest fear is she'll grow up to be a Hooters girl."

I nodded, thinking of my mother and how she must have felt watching all my potential strapping itself to the back of George's motorcycle.

"So you got a big day?" I asked, finishing my coffee and starting in on the pancakes.

"Yeah," she said. "I'm going down to the radio station."

"Radio station?" I asked.

She leaned forward, her voice quiet and excited. "I didn't want to say anything because I didn't want to jinx it, but I'm pitching a radio show." She giggled. And she hadn't cursed once all morning. I'd been too self-obsessed to notice the change in her until now.

"No way," I said, a stab of jealousy hitting me. I was the one with the wall full of sticky notes staring me down at night, and Elizabeth was the one whose life was changing. *No fair! No fair!* my inner child whined.

She laughed. "I started being straight with my clients about a week or so ago. You have no idea what it's done for me. I can breathe again."

Good for her. "Did any of them leave you?"

She shrugged. "One or two. Good riddance. But one of my clients referred me to her friend who is the promotions manager at that new all-talk AM station. We're meeting today to discuss me having my own show."

"Holy crap," I said, stabbing at my pancakes, willing my inner child to mature to the level of at least an inner preteen. "That's great." I hoped I sounded sincere, because part of me was. The part that was not a big baby and a rotten friend, that is.

"I really have you to thank," she said after a moment of silence.

"I didn't tell you anything you didn't already know."

"No," she said, "but you saw me standing on the ledge and you pushed me over. Thanks."

We looked at each other. It was a nice moment and at the

same time a little uncomfortable. Our friendship had been forged on the ground of each of us being bitter and angry. This change in Elizabeth might upset that balance.

"You're welcome," I said, shrugging. "I don't suppose you can return the favor and tell me why I'm hearing strands of phantom music?"

She stared at me for a moment. "Do something for me," she said, picking up her coffee mug and putting it in the sink. "If I get this radio gig, don't call in with that shit, okay?"

I smiled. Things with New Elizabeth were going to be just fine.

᭐᭐

Of all the sticky notes on my wall, *Get a job* was going to be the easiest to take care of. I stuffed it in the pocket of my jacket and got in my car to nab myself a free mocha and a face-to-face with Joe Bones. My biggest problem was trying to figure out a way to ask him if his job offer was still good without admitting that he'd been right and that lazing around like a damn dog had, in fact, been bad for me.

As it turned out, that little problem resolved itself.

"Wanda!" Shelley, all round with baby and glowing, waddled out from behind the counter when she saw me coming in from the coffee shop. Shelley was one of those people who loved being pregnant. Me, just looking at a pregnant woman made my back ache. I'll be buying little girls from China, thanks.

"Bones told me you came by last week. Sorry I missed you."

Shelley grabbed me and pulled me into a hug. I wasn't typically a huggy person, but I knew better than to argue with anyone in Bones's genetic line.

"Me, too," I said, lifting my mocha in salute. "I see you're knocked up again."

She rolled her eyes. "You been hanging out with Bones too much."

I grinned. "Where is the old goat, anyway? I need to talk to him."

"He's out visiting Dr. Macon, checking on the new hip."

"He okay?" I asked.

"Oh, please," she said, shaking her head and laughing. "I'm more worried about Doc Macon."

I laughed with her. "Yeah, I can see that. Mind if I wander around a bit till he gets in?"

"Fine by me, long as you buy something," she said with a smile, waving me away.

I checked out the self-help books first. Not a single one said anything about sticky notes. I wove my way through the lit section, running my fingers over the books. A glass case in the middle held the valuable and old titles. A first English edition of *Anna Karenina* caught my eye. I touched the glass and stared at it for a minute, until the music got my attention. It was Christmas music, and I was fairly sure it was real.

I smiled. The Grand Santa Station.

I first encountered the Station while shooting a spot for Bones last season. It was run by a guy named Charlie Dent, one of Bones's old war buddies. Even with my two-sizes-too-small heart, I had to admit Charlie had a rocking setup. There was a puppet show every hour on the hour, and a wooden train gave kids rides around the perimeter, dragged by elf-costumed college kids who couldn't get a better job for Christmas break.

Charlie was the perfect Santa, with his natural white beard and unnatural patience. Hell, he'd even put up with me when I sat on his lap last year and asked him for a dead ex-husband for Christmas. He'd laughed and said he'd do what he could for me. I liked Charlie. It would be good to see him again.

I turned a corner and stopped short. No train. No puppets. One little girl and her mother. One elf, a teenage kid dressed in a green tunic that was three sizes too big for her, snapping pictures on a cheap Polaroid. The Santa was not Charlie, but some younger, fatter, and balder guy who was gripping his Santa hat in his hand as he growled at the little girl.

"Come 'ere, kid," he said. The little girl tightened her grip on her mother's leg. I wasn't close enough to tell for sure, but it appeared that Santa'd been bathing in the hooch.

Santa rolled his eyes and stamped his foot. "I don't got all day, kid. Come 'ere, tell me what you want, and then you can go running to Mommy."

Excuse me? I crossed my arms and watched, hoping the mother would open up a can of whoop-ass on this guy. The mother flushed with anger, but the little girl was already walking over to Santa, so no whoop-ass. Instead, the mother paid the elf for the crappy Polaroid shot and ushered her daughter away. Hooch Claus jerked his chin at me with a tobacco-stained smile. "You wanna sit on Santa's lap, little girl?"

"Bite me, asshole," I said, then turned on my heel and went up to the front counter.

"Um, Shelley?" I called, waving her over to the end of the counter, away from the other customers. She waddled on over. "What's the deal with Santa?"

She rolled her eyes. "I know. I'm just waiting for Bones to get back to throw his sorry ass out." She put a protective hand on her stomach.

"Who is that guy?" I asked. "Where's Charlie?"

Her face darkened. "Charlie died last June. Didn't Bones tell you?"

I shook my head, but I wasn't surprised. Santa was dead. It seemed an appropriate comment on a generally sucky year.

Shelley crossed her arms and glared in the direction of the Grand Santa Station. "Lyle is Charlie's nephew and only living relative. He got everything, including the Station."

"Well, he has to go," I said. "He's scaring the kids."

Shelley nodded. "I know. The Station just opened up today, and by the time I got the chance to check things out, Bones was gone, and it's for damn sure I'm not putting my pregnant ass within ten feet of that man."

"Wait a minute." I looked at the calendar on the wall behind her. "Doesn't that stuff usually start after Thanksgiving?"

She shrugged and rolled her eyes. "Lyle came in this morning determined to start it up. I'm guessing he's hard up for cash. Even cheap whiskey is hard to afford when you're a *loser!*"

She shouted the "loser" part in Lyle's general direction. Nothing came back.

"Lyle owns the Station now?"

Shelley nodded. "Yeah. We don't owe him the space or anything, so I guess we'll either buy him out or give him everything and send him on his way."

Hmm. I cocked my head to the side as some creaky gears began to churn. "How much do you think it's worth?"

Shelley eyed me for a second. "I can't remember exactly," she said, "but I think it's somewhere in the neighborhood of seven grand."

"Seven grand?" I said. "For that? Are you kidding me?"

She shrugged. "Well, there are the costumes and the photography equipment for collateral, along with the trains and puppet show. Most of that stuff's still in the basement because Lyle's a *lazy bastard.*" Again, with the shouting. Again, no response. She turned her attention back to me. "And then there's the earning potential, which actually isn't bad in a good season."

I raised an eyebrow at her. "Really? How not bad is it?"

She smiled. "Why you asking, Wanda?"

"Would you be surprised if I told you I had several thousand dollars burning a hole in my bank account?"

Shelley laughed. "Wanda, nothing you say surprises me. You know that."

I nodded and patted her hand. "Wait right here."

She shook her head and waved me on. "Call me if you need backup."

I charged back to the Santa Station and arrived just as a little boy was running away, crying, with his mother following after him. There were no other children around. I walked up to Lyle and put my hands on either side of his Santa throne, pinning him in.

He grinned up at me. "I knew you'd be back." His breath was an offensive combination of hot schnapps and day-old pizza, but I didn't flinch.

"Listen to me, you pathetic little piece of reindeer shit, I'm gonna cut to the chase. I'll give you six thousand dollars right here, right now, if you sign this business over to me and leave immediately."

He turned his eyes to slits and looked at me sideways, jutting his chin up. "'Sworth seven."

"You're not getting seven. You're getting six. Just think about how many bars you can get thrown out of with that kind of cash."

He looked from side to side. I don't know if he was trying to see if anyone was watching, or if he was looking for an escape, but either way, he wasn't getting up until I got what I wanted.

He let out a small belch. I tried not to recoil. "You telling me you got six thousand dollars? Right here? Right now?"

"If you've got the business license, I've got six thousand dollars. Right here. Right now."

Twenty minutes later Lyle was heading out the front door with a check for six thousand of my dollars stuffed in his pocket, and I was putting on an oversize Santa suit and introducing myself to my new employee, a teenage elf named Anne Marie.

"You played Santa all day?" Kacey asked. She'd been sitting in the kitchen doing her homework when I came in at nine-thirty. I had my wine bottle opened and was pouring a drink before I even noticed she was there.

"Yeah," I said. "I was. How'd you know?"

"Mom mentioned it when you weren't at dinner." She scribbled something in her notebook, then rubbed it out with the eraser. "How was it?"

"Okay," I said, "but there's a lot of work to do. I need to hire some Santas and some elves, and then I need to do something about the camera."

"What's the matter with it?" she asked.

"It's this crappy old Polaroid," I said. "The film keeps getting jammed. Think you might be able to fix it for me?"

"Probably," she said, shrugging. "But you'll be better off getting a digital camera and a laptop. You can do some cool stuff with that."

I sat down next to her at the table. "Really? Like what?"

She flipped her book shut. "Borders around the edges. Cool themes. That kind of stuff."

I nodded. I had no idea what the hell she was talking about. "Think you might be able to help me with that?"

"Sure. PowerBooks are the coolest. Get a red one. Do you really hear music in your head?"

I rolled my eyes. "Your mom tell you that, too?"

She shook her head. "Nope. Alex overheard you guys talking."

I sighed. "Yeah, I hear music in my head."

"What music?"

"I don't know. Do you ever run out of questions?"

"How does it go?"

"Why do you want to know?"

"Maybe I know it."

I patted her hand. "It's not by Justin Timberlake."

She patted my hand back, mocking the condescending manner in which I'd done it to her. I liked this kid. "Alex said you thought it was classical. I listen to classical music, too."

I sat back and gave her a cynical look. "Name two classical composers. Beethoven, Bach, and Mozart don't count."

"Rachmaninoff. Berlioz. Handel. Tchaikovsky."

I held up a hand. "I said two."

I stared at her for a moment and finally decided that I had nothing to lose, and there was a chance it could kill a sticky note. I hummed the crescendo—as well as I could, anyway. I wasn't exactly tone-deaf, but you wouldn't wanna hear me do "Honesty" on Karaoke Night.

She shook her head. "Don't know it."

"Okay. Are we done with the grilling?"

"No. Can I be an elf?"

I shook my head. "I think there are laws against a kid your age working."

"Can I have some wine?"

"I *know* there are laws against that," I said. "Where's your mom?"

"She's in the tub," Kacey said, flipping her book back open. "She's crying."

I put down my glass. "Why? Is she okay? Did something happen? Where's Alex?" I glanced around, in panic mode.

"Everything's fine. Alex is at Dad's tonight." She gave me an appraising look. I could practically hear the gears in her twelve-year-old mind trying to decide if I was to be trusted with the family skeletons. Apparently, I passed muster.

"It's not a big deal. Whenever Dad comes to get one of us, Mom locks herself in the bathroom and cries. She thinks I don't know."

"But you know everything," I said, finishing the thought. "Why aren't you at your dad's tonight?"

She rolled her eyes. "Dad read some self-help book about kids needing special one-on-one time. Alex goes on Friday nights, I go on Saturdays, and then we all do something together on Sundays." She paused, waiting to be sure she had my attention before she dropped the next bomb. "Like that makes up for him cheating on my mom."

I stared her down. "This is not a confirmation, but how do you know about that?"

Kacey rolled her eyes again. Rolling eyes seemed to be very big with her. "Why do grown-ups assume that being twelve means you're stupid?"

"I don't think anybody would ever call you stupid, Kace," I said. She pushed her glasses up on her nose and smiled at me. I felt a small lurch in my heart, and I had a strange urge to wrap my arms around her and kiss the top of her head.

Christ. I stood up and refilled my glass of wine. *Develop a maternal instinct* was not on my wall, and I had enough to worry about right now without some kid making my uterus ache.

She put her pencil down in her book and closed it. "Are people always intimidated by intelligent women?"

I smiled. "Not the good ones."

She nodded. "Can I have some wine now?"

I walked over to her and handed her my glass. "One sip," I said. "And don't tell your mother."

෴

I crawled into bed at midnight, two hours after I sent Kacey to bed. I briefly considered going up and forcing Elizabeth to talk but decided against it. Instead, I busied myself in the kitchen on the off chance that she might come down. She never did, but I went to bed hoping she'd be pleasantly surprised to see her spices alphabetically organized the next time she went looking for oregano.

I pulled the covers up to my ears and let my eyes float over the sticky-note wall, taking in all the crooked demands one by one.

Get a new haircut.

Go see parents.

Talk to Molly.

Do something meaningful.

Identify phantom music.

Figure out what I want.

I stared at them, reading them over and over again, until my eyes finally rested on the one that was set apart from the others, the one that would stay there until all the others were gone.

Tell Walter.

I bunched my pillow under my head and hugged it, falling asleep to thoughts of seeing Walter again and showing him who I really was. Of course, I'd have to figure that out for myself first. Details sucked.

"Is Elizabeth here?"

Jack Mackey was a tall man, handsome, with a winning smile and a firm handshake. Under ordinary circumstances, I probably would have liked him. As it was, I stood in the door-way with my arms crossed, ready to use deadly force if he tried to get near Elizabeth.

"No," I said. "I told her I'd handle the switch this morning."

"Oh." He rocked back on his heels. He smiled, held out his hand. "I'm Jack. I take it you're Wanda? The kids have been telling me about you."

My eyes flicked from his outstretched hand back to his face. I kept my arms crossed. "Did they tell you I'm not into small talk?"

His head turned slightly, and his eyes locked on me, seeming to sense a challenge. "No. As a matter of fact, they've had nothing but nice things to say about you. They really like you."

I threw a holler over my shoulder without taking my eyes off Jack. "Kace! You ready yet, kiddo?"

"Almost," she called down. I could hear the sound of Alex's

stereo bound down the stairs, then retreat as he shut the door to his bedroom.

Jack kept his eyes on me. "You know, I'm not really the asshole Elizabeth says I am."

"The only thing Elizabeth has told me is that you're a good father to the kids," I said. "I put two and two together and came up with asshole all by myself."

Kacey's footsteps pounded behind me, and I uncrossed my arms to give her a quick hug and send her off with Jack.

"It was nice meeting you," Jack said. I put on a smile for Kacey's benefit and nodded, watching them as they headed to the car. He held Kacey's hand and buckled her in gently, giving her a kiss on the forehead before closing the door and going around to get in on the driver's side. Once they were gone, I went upstairs and woke up Elizabeth to tell her that Alex was home, Kacey was gone, and I was heading out to play Santa.

❧

"Holy Christ, if I have to make nice to one more damn kid today, I'm gonna lose my damn mind," I said, slamming my Santa hat down on Bones's desk as I took a long drink of my bottled water. The uterus ache from the night before had all but been obliterated by a series of selfish little brats demanding PlayStations and swing sets. I yanked open the top of my Santa coat. "I'm sweating bullets in this damn suit."

"Don't come bitching to me," Bones said. "I didn't ask you to buy the Station."

"Nice gratitude," I said, "after I saved your sorry ass from a probable lawsuit."

Bones looked up at the clock. "Isn't your break over yet?"

I settled in the comfy chair across from his desk. "I got ten more minutes."

"There's a break room in the back for employees," he said.

"Good thing I'm not your employee."

He made a dismissive noise and turned his attention to the mail on his desk. I smiled. Although playing Santa pretty much sucked, I had to admit that having something to do with my days was improving my general mood. The fact that I got to irritate Bones while doing it was pure gravy.

I watched him go through his mail, quietly drinking my water and fanning myself with a manila folder I'd pulled off his filing cabinet. My eyes floated over the items on his desk: a blotter, a pencil sharpener, a letter opener.

A package of sticky notes.

Crap. I sighed, closed my eyes, and saw my wall full of crooked notes taunting me. If things were going to change, I was going to have to make them change. I sucked in some breath and spoke.

"Hey, Bones?"

"Hmph?" he grunted, not looking up from the mail.

I got stuck on what I wanted to say, then rolled my eyes at myself. *Go ahead, Wanda. Have an adult conversation. You might like it.*

"Have you . . . always known . . . what you wanted?"

Bones's eyes stopped focusing on the letter he was reading,

but it took a moment before they floated up to me. "What kind of damn fool question is that?"

I bopped my head back and forth on my shoulders, trying to think of an answer that didn't include the phrase *Bite me.*

"I just . . ." I sighed. Why was this so hard? "I'm going through a thing . . . right now . . . and I'm trying to figure out what I want. Out—out of life."

Bones watched me carefully, as though I were a dog and he didn't know whether to pet or kick me. In the end he did neither.

"You in therapy or something?" he asked. "That sounds like a question someone in therapy might ask."

"No, I'm not in therapy." *Not technically.* "I'm just . . . I'm trying to figure things out. Forget I asked. You're too damn cranky to be of any use to me, anyway."

I took a swig of my water, preparing a wiseass comment if he poked fun at how red my face was.

"What are you doing for Thanksgiving?"

I looked up. "What?"

He flattened his palms against the desktop. "Thanksgiving. Next Thursday. Don't you ever look at a damn calendar?"

I gave a pointed glance at the calendar over his shoulder, then back at him. "No."

He sat back and crossed his arms over his chest. "Shelley wants you to spend it with us, if you don't have plans."

"I do," I lied. "Have plans, I mean."

He gave a short nod, then picked up his letter, although he kept his eyes on me. "You okay, Wanda?"

"Yeah. I'm fine. I have plans. My break's over."

He waved his fingers at me. "On with you, then."

I turned around, got to the door, turned back, grabbed my water, caught Bones watching me with smiling eyes.

"Oh, bite me, Bones," I said, slamming the door behind me and giving myself and my maturity an internal pat on the back. *You go, girl.*

"What are you doing for Thanksgiving?" Elizabeth handed me a plate to dry.

"I can't believe you don't have a damn dishwasher," I said, running my dampened towel over yet another plate.

"You know," she said, an amused smile playing on her lips, "I take back everything I ever said about you not having the right disposition to play Santa."

I put the plate away. "I've got some guy Santas starting after the holiday. And not a moment too soon."

She laughed and was quiet for a minute. "So do you have plans for Thanksgiving?"

"Yes," I lied. "What is this obsession everyone has with Thanksgiving?"

Elizabeth eyed me. "It's Thursday."

"I know."

She rinsed a bowl and handed it to me. "The kids and I are leaving Wednesday to visit my sister Cheryl in Atlanta. She invited you to come along."

"Thanks," I said, giving a flat smile. "Can't. Plans."

"I see," she said. "You haven't asked me about my meeting with the radio people."

"Oh. Crap. Yeah. How was your meeting with the radio people?"

"Great." She turned off the water and dried her hands on the kitchen towel. "I'm meeting with the station manager on Tuesday."

"That's terrific." I meant it. I was genuinely happy for her. Too bad *Grow up just a tiny bit* wasn't on a sticky note on my wall, or I'd feel like I'd actually accomplished something that day.

"Well, if you change your mind about Thanksgiving," she said.

"Can't. Plans."

She nodded. "Yeah. Thanks for helping with the dishes."

I smiled. "Least I can do."

"Well. Good night," she said, heading out of the kitchen. I stood there alone for a few minutes, then turned out the light and went up to my room.

෨෨

I had just put my feet up on Elizabeth's coffee table, a Marie Callender's turkey dinner on my lap and a glass of good ol' Albert on ice nearby, when I heard the noise. My heart kicked up a notch. I hit the mute button on the remote, shushing Frasier and Niles, and sat frozen on the couch, listening.

Nothing.

I took a sip of my drink but didn't feel any better. It would be just like George to fuck up a perfectly fine Thanksgiving.

I put my meal down and glanced at the door: it was locked. All the window shades were drawn. If he was out there, he wouldn't be able to see me. I could run to the phone in the kitchen and dial 911, and the cops would probably get there before he killed me.

Probably.

Or they could show up, discover the noise was the neighbor's cat—or, worse, my imagination—and I'd die of humiliation. Either way, it sucked to be me.

Crack. I jumped up off the couch. It sounded like the crack of a piece of wood, maybe a large twig under someone's foot. Or a revolver cocking.

"Revolver," I huffed at myself. (A) How the hell would I know what a cocking revolver sounded like? (B) It was a twig.

Under a foot.

Crap. How could he have found me? Had he been watching me all along? Had he been waiting to make his move until after Elizabeth and the kids left? But they'd been gone since the day before; why wait until now?

I opened the front hall closet and pulled out Alex's aluminum baseball bat. I went into the kitchen and got the cordless off the wall. Hauling the bat over my shoulder, I walked up to the door. I flicked on the porch light and looked through the peephole at the same time.

"Wanda? Is that you?"

I screamed long and hard, releasing the pent-up terror lurking in my chest. Then I opened the door and threw the bat at Jack, who ducked as it went whizzing by his head.

"Wanda!" He looked over his shoulder as the bat landed on the lawn. "I'm sorry. Did I scare you?"

"Did you . . . did you . . . *scare* me? No, Jack. You freaked the living shit out of me. I'm going to have to go change my underwear now." I bent over, both palms on my knees, and gasped for breath. "What the hell did you think you were doing?"

"I was driving by to check on the place. I thought you'd gone with Elizabeth and the kids. When I saw the lights on . . ."

"Did she *ask* you to check up on the place?"

He shrugged. "No, I just thought . . ."

I straightened up. "Jesus, Jack. If you'd been that attentive before, you might still be married."

His face hardened. He stepped back. "Look, I'm sorry I scared you. I'll go."

I held up my hands. "No, you totally freaked me out, you're staying until I calm down." I grabbed my jacket off the coat-rack. "Do you smoke, Jack?"

"I haven't smoked since Elizabeth got pregnant with Alex," Jack said, blowing a smoke ring into the chilled air. He took a sip of his Scotch and sat back in the porch chair.

"Ah," I said, "count yourself among the many who have fallen under the bad influence of Wanda Lane."

I stubbed my cigarette out in the cracked saucer we were using for an ashtray, exhaling my last bit of smoke into the night. "What are you doing here, Jack?"

"I told you," he said. "I was checking on the house."

"No," I said. "That was an hour ago. Why are you sitting here, on Thanksgiving, smoking cigarettes with a stranger? Why aren't you with your biddy?"

He looked away from his smoke rings. "Biddy?"

I gave him cynical eyes. "You expect me to believe that a guy who couldn't keep it in his pants while he was married is biddyless now that he's single? That's a hard line to sell, Jack."

He shook his head. "You never let up, do you?"

"On a typical day, no."

"Fine. Fair's fair. The kids told me you were invited to go to Cheryl's. What are *you* doing here drinking and smoking alone on Thanksgiving?"

I pulled a fresh cigarette from the pack. "I'm not alone. You're here."

"You know what I mean."

I shrugged. "I'm not into holidays."

He nodded, took another drink. There was a long pause, then, "There's no hope for me, is there?"

I sighed, knowing exactly what he was talking about. "Personally, I think your last chance ran out the door stuck to the naked ass of Ms. Hastings Flowers. But my opinion doesn't matter because I'm not the one who decides what Elizabeth wants."

"Yeah," he said, leaning back. "I know."

"And it occurs to me," I said, because I just couldn't resist poking at a sore spot, "that if you really want Elizabeth back, you could start by dropping the lawsuit against her."

He rubbed his hands over his face. "Yeah. I know. It's just . . . She wouldn't talk to me . . ."

"So . . . you thought you'd win her favor by suing her and forcing her to see you in court?" I snorted out a laugh. "I hate to be the one to break it to you, man, but you definitely are stupider than you look."

He leaned forward, elbows on his knees, and stared out into the night. "You may not believe this, but I'm not a bad guy. I'm a stupid guy. I love Elizabeth. I love my kids." He paused. "I didn't even like Ms. Hastings Flowers."

There was a long silence. I thought he was done. I was wrong.

"I guess I was so scared of losing everything that I just threw it all away on purpose. Like I said, stupid."

I looked over at him. His face was tight, his eyes radiating misery. As much as I didn't want to admit it, Jack Mackey and I were two peas in a pod.

"For what it's worth, Jack," I said, "I don't think it's hopeless. I'm not saying you don't have a lot to make up for, but I don't think it's hopeless."

He raised his eyes to me, looked over his shoulder and then back at me with a sly smile. "I'm sorry, Wanda, is that you? Are you being nice to me? Did the laws of nature just reverse or what?"

I raised my glass. "For both of our sakes, let's hope so."

We toasted, and each of us drank, then sat together in silence, two people bonded by stupidity.

8

"Forgive me, Father, but I'm still screwed up." I leaned back in the confessional and rested my head against the wall, looking up all the way to the cathedral ceiling. It hadn't occurred to me that there wouldn't be a top on the confessional box. Maybe that was so the confession could drift right on up to God. Maybe it was so the confessional wouldn't be too dark. Maybe it was so the parish could afford those rocking stained-glass windows.

"Do I know you?"

I picked my head up and looked at the grate. "You might not remember me. I'm Wanda, the woman who's not Catholic? Came in here talking about how my horrible ex-husband drove my family away? You were really mean to me and made me cry? Told me to do something meaningful?"

"Oh." I could practically hear him smiling. "Yes. Any chance you're actually going to join the church someday and make this clandestine relationship of ours official?"

Clandestine. Vocab points for Father Hard-Ass. "Do you think that would help me?"

"Why would I think that?"

I smiled. "It's kinda dead out there today, Father. I didn't see a single other sinner when I came in. I thought y'all might be closed."

"It's the day after Thanksgiving. They're all at the mall."

"Ah." I paused. The father coughed. A beat. Then—

"Wanda? You still there?"

"Yeah. I'm just thinking."

"Well, it's your dime, but since you're here, you might as well think out loud."

Okay. "Have you always known what you wanted, Father?"

That seemed to take him by surprise. He paused, then came back with, "I'm not sure I know what you mean."

"Well, being a priest is a pretty big commitment."

"You could say that."

"Did you always know? That it was what you wanted out of life?"

Another pause. "Are we talking about me?"

"No." I sighed and leaned my head back, staring up at the cathedral ceiling and performing a conversational free fall. "I just . . . I'm going through this thing right now. There's this guy, this wonderful man who cares about me for God knows what reason . . . and then there are a bunch of sticky notes I have to go through . . . and I keep hearing this music that no one else can hear . . . It's a long story. I guess what it all comes down to is that I'm trying to figure out what I want out of life, and I'm not getting anywhere. I'll be honest with you, I'm a little frustrated."

"Well, if it's any comfort, that's not an easy question for anybody to answer."

"Yeah, I know," I said. "Blah, blah, blah."

I heard him huff through the grate. "You know, there's a rabbi down the street who has office hours on Fridays."

"You trying to get rid of me?"

"No, not at all."

"Good, because I have another question for you."

"That's what I'm here for."

"This whole 'Do something meaningful' thing. What did you mean by that?"

"I think it's pretty self-explanatory."

"I'm not that clever, Father."

He chuckled. It echoed off the small space and lifted upward. I was beginning to like the confessional. "I doubt that."

"It's just that I don't—thank you—I don't know what to do. My friend and her ex-husband are still in love with each other. There's a lot of bad water under the bridge, but they've got these great kids, and I think, you know, if I can help them get back together, then that would be meaningful, right?"

Silence.

"Right?" I asked again. Father Hard-Ass was being a little slow on the uptake.

"Well," he said, "getting involved in other people's relationships can be big trouble. Especially if they don't want you involved."

I sighed. "Yeah, that's what I thought, too, but I'm really desperate to do something meaningful."

Pause. "Then it seems like you have a choice to make."

Well, duh. "Yes. That's why I'm here."

"Why?"

"So you can tell me what I should do."

"What makes you think I know what you should do?"

"Well, I figure a priest won't let me do the wrong thing."

"This is why people need to join the church before going to confession. I'm here to listen to your sins, not to make all your choices for you."

Now, there was the Father Hard-Ass I knew and loved. "Look, I'm just trying to do the right thing. Tell me what to do, and I'll do it."

"All right. Join the church."

We both laughed. "No, Father. I mean about the something meaningful. Should I do it? Do the ends justify the means?"

"That all depends on the ends and the means."

I threw my hands up in the air. "For crying out loud! Do I have to join the church to get a straight answer outta you?"

"Yes!" He laughed again, then paused. When he started talking, his voice was more serious. "What you need to do is between you and God. And I'm not privy to that information, even if you join the church." A beat. "But it can't hurt to hedge your bets."

I grinned. "A couple of Hail Marys, then?"

"We'll get to that. For now, I think you should go to the gift shop and buy a St. Erasmus medal."

"A St. what medal?"

"Erasmus. Also known as St. Elmo."

"Oh," I said, brightening. "The guy from *St. Elmo's Fire*?"

Father Hard-Ass sighed. I imagined he got that a lot. "The lights in the sky that used to help sailors find their way were named after him, yes. He's the patron saint of navigators. Maybe he can help you find your way."

I could feel my throat tighten with emotion. *Cripes*. What was the deal with me? Getting weepy over a saint? I should trade in all those sticky notes for a prescription and get it over with. I stood up.

"Thanks." I looked up at the ornate cathedral ceiling again. "Hey, Father? I know this is supposed to be all confidential and everything, but can I know your name?"

There was a pause. Then, "I'm Father Gregory."

"Nice to meet you, Father Gregory. I'm Wanda."

I heard a chuckle. "It was nice meeting you, too, Wanda."

I nodded, even though I knew he couldn't see it. I grabbed at the curtain but paused before leaving. "Father Gregory?"

"Yes?"

"Thank you. For listening to me. Even though I'm not part of your flock."

He leaned close to the grate and spoke in a low, friendly tone. "Don't tell anyone, but I've enjoyed listening to you."

I smiled. Had me a priest on my team. That had to be a good sign. "Maybe I'll see you again sometime."

"I'm here all week. Be sure to tip your waitress."

I went straight from there to the gift shop. They were all out of St. Erasmus medals. Shocker.

"Just shut up and sit down," I said. "And put the damn hat on, will you?"

Bones grumbled something offensive but put the hat on. "What time is it?" he asked. "I'm already hotter 'n hell in this getup."

I checked my watch. "Eight-forty-five. Fifteen minutes to open."

I checked the connection from the digital camera on the tripod to the computer, then went around the desk to check out the image in the software Kacey had set up for me. I hit the button to take the picture, and the flash lit up Bones's craggy old face.

"Damn, girl, you trying to blind me?" he yelled. "I don't know who ever heard of a black damn Santa Claus, anyway."

"You don't shut up, Bones," I said, bringing the printout over to show him, "you're gonna be a dead damn Santa Claus."

He took the printout from me. It was good quality, on card stock, with a mistletoe border that read "Merry Christmas" in the lower right-hand corner. He harrumphed and handed it back to me.

"It's off-center."

"You're off-center," I grumbled, heading back to the computer but freezing midway.

"Bones? Is that music playing on the system?"

"What music?" *Damn.* The crescendo built. I hummed along, closed my eyes, tried to place it.

"What's wrong with you, Wanda?"

I held up a hand to shush Bones. The music faded. *Shit.* I

continued over to the computer, only looking up after I realized Bones had been uncommonly silent.

"What?" I said.

"You going crazy on me, girl?" he asked.

"Just a little," I said. "No more than usual."

He nodded but continued to watch me, his dark eyes glittering with poorly masked concern.

"Stop eyeballing me, Bones," I said. "I'm fine."

He looked away, tugging at the collar of the Santa suit. "Don't think I'm gonna be doing this Santa thing for you every damn day. I have real work to do, you know."

I grinned. "Just smile and look pretty, Bones. Only six more hours to go."

"Have you spoken to Jack lately?"

Elizabeth stopped dunking her tea bag. I took a sip of my coffee and tried to look casual.

"No," she said, and continued dunking. "Why?"

"No reason," I said, shrugging. "Can I ask you something?"

"Sure."

"Do you still love him?"

She gave me a tight smile. "Are you ever going to call Walter or what?"

Oooh. Counterattack. I raised my eyebrows and pulled an Elizabeth. "We were talking about Walter?"

"No," she said, then threw her hands up in the air. "Don't you have Santa pictures to take?"

I shook my head. "Monday. Station's closed. Deft change of subject, by the way. Now back to you and Jack."

"Why are you suddenly so interested in me and Jack?" She white-knuckled her tea mug and took a sip. I half expected the thing to crack in her hands.

"He came by to check on the house on Thanksgiving. We talked."

"Wait. You were here on Thanksgiving? I thought you had plans."

"They fell through. Anyway, we talked and . . ." I cleared my throat. "He still loves you, Elizabeth."

She put the mug down and put her face in her hands. "I can't talk about this, Wanda."

"Okay," I said. "That's okay. Look, I don't know anything about anything, but he seemed sincere to me. I just thought you should know."

She slammed her hands down on the table. I jumped back.

"I know," she said, her voice taut with anger. "I know he loves me. I know he's out there being all hurt and sorry and . . ." She took a deep breath. Her eyes welled up. "You wanna know if I love him? Yes, I love him. And maybe he still loves me. And maybe he's changed, but I'm not going to destroy myself again on a maybe. I'd rather be alone forever than go through that again."

She stood up and poured her tea down the drain. I kept my back to her, feeling like the stupidest person alive, hearing my father's voice ring out in my head: *Sometimes you just have to know when to shut the hell up.*

"I'm sorry," I said. "I shouldn't have said anything."

She sighed. I turned around and looked at her. In four minutes she'd aged five years.

"No, I'm sorry," she said, rubbing her forehead. "It's just . . . You're right. You don't know about me and Jack. Just like I don't know what's going on with you and Walter, but I stay out of it because it's not my business."

I nodded. "Well, actually, you have kind of butted in on it once or twice."

She raised one eyebrow at me. "You looking for a fight?"

I smiled. "As I'm pretty sure you'd kick my ass, I'd have to say no."

She walked over to me and put her hand on my shoulder. "I appreciate that you cared enough to talk to me about it."

I grinned at her. "No, you don't. You wanna pull my damn hair out."

She grinned back. "Not all of it."

I glanced at my watch and stood up. "On that note, I have to run."

She sat down at the table and grabbed the paper. "I thought today was your day off."

"It is," I said, grabbing my jacket off the coatrack. "But, thanks to you, I've got a wall full of sticky notes that aren't resolving themselves."

She smiled and waved me away. "Go do something meaningful, then."

๑๑

The Randall P. McKay Shelter for Men was a small place downtown that was stuffed between a gay nightclub and the offices for the *Hastings Daily Reporter*. I walked in the front door and found an older woman sitting at a desk, her arms wrapping a sweater tightly around her. Some shelter. It wasn't any warmer inside the place than it was outside.

I handed her one of the color sheets I'd made at the Kinko's down the street. "Hi, my name is Wanda . . ." I looked down at the ID tag hanging around her neck. ". . . Karen. I'm running the Grand Santa Station over at Osgiliath Books, and I need some Santas."

Karen took the paper from me and skimmed it over, then handed it back. "Oh, honey. You don't want to come here."

I gave a tight smile. "If I didn't want to come here, then I wouldn't be here. I'm just trying to give an opportunity for a little work."

She shook her head. "I appreciate it, honey, really, it's a nice thought, but I'm not going to post that here. These guys are not the guys you want around kids. Trust me."

I sighed. She was probably right. But after my flaming crash-and-burn with Elizabeth that morning, giving jobs to down-and-outs was the only meaningful thing I'd come up with. Turns out, doing something meaningful was a massive pain in the ass.

"So there's no one here who needs a job, then?" I said. Before she could answer, I felt myself thrown forward over her desk.

"Hey, watch it!" I snapped, turning to see what big buffoon

was plowing through the Randall P. McKay Shelter for Men. "Well, I'll be damned."

"Who the fuck are you?" Lyle's eyes widened, then narrowed, then widened again. "Do I know you?"

"Told you," Karen said, picking up her newspaper.

Lyle pointed his finger at me, wobbling forward slightly and then doubling back. "I know you."

"Six grand goes fast, huh, Lyle?" I said. I took the paper back from Karen and gave her a smile. "I think you're right. Thanks for your help."

I stepped outside and hurried away from the shelter. I paused briefly outside the *Hastings Daily Reporter* office, then pushed my way inside. The girl at the front desk was hanging up the phone as I stepped in. She turned to me and smiled.

"Can I help you?" she asked.

"Yes," I said. "I'm looking for Jennifer, in classified ads. She owes me a favor, and I'm here to collect."

๑๑

One Santa ad and three errands later, I pulled into the parking lot at Hastings Channel 8. I didn't want to go in, almost turned around and drove out without stopping, but the day had been a bust in regards to sticky notes. I had to start making some progress.

I pushed through the double glass doors. Someone I didn't recognize was sitting at the front desk. Not a shock. Turnaround at Channel 8 tended to be speedy, and the receptionists whirled in and out of that place so fast I was surprised they didn't get whiplash.

"Hi, I'm Wanda Lane. I'm here to see Cate Manton." I flashed the new receptionist my most brilliant smile. She looked up at me and cracked her gum, staring vapidly at me. I cleared my throat and spoke slower and louder.

"Is Cate in today?"

"Damn straight she is!" Two firm hands grabbed my shoulders and pulled me into a hug. Cate was a tall woman, of solid German stock. I believe the term used most often to describe her was *brick shithouse*.

She turned to the receptionist. "It's okay, Marguerite. She's with me."

As Cate dragged me by the arm into her office, I heard the receptionist say, "My name is Heather." Cate either didn't notice or didn't care, so I let it go. Sometimes it's easier to pretend you didn't hear something. Heather'd be working somewhere else in a week or two, anyway.

"You are not going to believe what's been going on here," Cate gushed as she shut the door behind her. I held up my hand.

"I don't want to know."

"Sure you do. Blaine got fired."

My mouth dropped. "You're kidding! How did that happen?"

Cate grinned. "His dad was so pissed off after you filed the lawsuit that he canned him."

I shook my head. "I didn't file a lawsuit."

"You didn't? Word has it they paid you fifty grand to shut you up."

I rolled my eyes. "Do I look like anyone gave me fifty grand?" I reached into my purse and pulled out the package I'd just picked up at the novelty store. "I'm walking around with elf ears in my purse, for Christ's sake."

She checked out the ears and made a minor attempt to mask her concern. "Oh, sweetie, you need to come back."

"No way, Cate. That's not why I'm here. Look, I need your help."

"Oh, sure, but seriously . . ." She pulled her eyes away from the bag of ears but still looked concerned. "You need to come back. Things are so much better since Blaine left."

I held up my hands. "Waste of time, Catie. You can only sell television for so long before you lose your self-respect."

"Since when did you have any self-respect?" she asked with a grin. Her eyes dropped back to the package of ears and her smile faded. I grabbed them and shoved them back in my purse. She leaned forward. "Seriously, honey, what's up with the ears?"

"Nothing's up with the ears. Do you remember Molly Zane? I need to find her. I thought you might have an address on file. You know, where you sent her last check to, something like that."

Cate sat back and folded her arms across her chest. "You know it's illegal for me to share that information with you."

"I know, and I'm sorry to ask, but I really need—"

She laughed. "Oh, shut up. I'll get it for you. You just owe me, is all."

I grinned. "Don't you ever change, Cate."

She rummaged through her keys and walked over to the filing cabinet in the corner of her office. "I wouldn't dream of it."

〇〇

"Wanda?" I froze as I heard Walter's voice saying my name. I dropped the pen I'd been using to scratch down information from my home messages and sat down at Elizabeth's kitchen table, holding the phone tight to my ear.

"Elizabeth told me you're okay. I hope that's true. I just . . . I hope I didn't . . . Agh." He grunted in frustration. I felt my lunch rise in my throat. "If you just need time, I can respect that. If it's something that I've done, I wish you would tell me. Tony hasn't located your ex-husband yet, and I'm . . . concerned. Please, call me."

In my defense, I did call. I called and I let it ring and he answered the phone and I heard his voice and I started to cry and I hung up like a big stupid cowardly stupid baby.

But I called.

〇〇

"How's it going here, Kace?" I ambled up behind Kacey and placed a pile of burgers and fries and sodas on the desk next to the computer at the Santa Station. Kacey looked up at me and pulled the headphones out of her ears, turning off the portable CD player in her lap. "You say something, Wanda?"

"If that's 'Nsync, I'm gonna have a fit," I said. "Remind me to get you a Huey Lewis CD for your birthday."

She crinkled her nose at me. "No."

"Wise guy." I glanced past her at an unfamiliar screen on the computer. "What are you up to here?"

"Sit down. You're gonna love this." I sat down in the seat next to her and she turned to me, wringing her hands in excitement. "I've worked out a system."

"A system?" I said, grabbing a fry out of the bag. "How long was I gone? Twenty minutes?"

"Well, I've been thinking about it for a while. I've just implemented it today." *Implemented.* Gotta love a kid who uses words like *implemented.*

"This is how it works. Anne Marie"—she pointed to Anne Marie, who was working the train—"chats with the kids while she pulls the train. She gets the names, favorite colors, stuff like that."

I leaned back over the computer, and Kacey pointed to the child on Bones's lap. "I also rigged up a baby monitor. Hope you don't mind I used some of the petty cash." She picked up the receiving end and turned up the volume, and we eavesdropped on Bones talking to the little girl on his lap.

"You been studying your letters?" he asked her. She nodded without saying a word, in awe of Santa Bones.

"You can talk, can'tcha?" Bones asked her. She nodded again.

"Well, I can't hear ya, but I'm very, very old, and sometimes you have to shout with old men like me," he said.

I smiled, watching him with that little girl, and felt a swell of emotion for the old goat. Kacey raised her hand and made a gesture to Bones, which he acknowledged with a slight nod.

"So what is it you want for Christmas this year, Isabelle?"

"I want a Barbie," Isabelle said. I slapped my hand against my forehead.

"Barbie!" I stage-whispered to Kacey. "For crying out loud, what's the deal with the friggin' Barbies?"

"I know," Kacey said, shaking her head. "Did you know that if Barbie was a real woman with those proportions, she'd have to carry her kidneys in her purse?"

I laughed. "Your mom is going to regret letting you guys hang out with me after school. You're turning into a full-fledged wiseass."

She grinned but didn't turn her eyes away from the keyboard. "I have a whole bunch of themes based on the most popular requests." She bit her lip as she tapped on the keyboard. "And here's . . . Barbie."

I checked out the computer screen as the normal, generic Christmas border that we printed on the pictures was replaced by a Barbie Christmas theme.

"Wow," I said.

"And that's not all. We've got a ton of them. There are dog themes, cat themes, arts and crafts, NASCAR. And if you're in a pinch, just generic girl and boy themes."

"You created all those?"

Kacey shook her head. "I downloaded them off of the Internet on Mom's computer at home. Didn't you know this software has a Web site?"

"A what site?"

Kacey sighed and continued clacking on the keyboard and

snapped her fingers at me to take the picture of Isabelle with Bones. I shot the picture, and by the time I got back, Kacey had inserted a note for Isabelle in the corner of the Barbie theme and was sending it to the printer.

She swirled around in the office chair and looked at me. Her feet didn't even touch the floor. "What do you think?"

I picked up the printout. The border was pink, and Barbie stood in the corner, with a speech balloon coming out of her mouth that said "Merry Christmas, Isabelle!"

"I think it's incredible." As I spoke, Anne Marie got the picture from me and inserted it in the cardboard frame. She winked at Kacey. "Kid sure runs a tight ship."

Isabelle and her mother took the picture from Anne Marie, gushing over it as they headed for the children's-books section. Anne Marie headed back to work the train, and Bones had another kid on his lap.

"Damn," I said. "I'm finding it increasingly hard to believe you're only twelve."

She laughed. "I'm an old soul."

I resisted an impulse to ruffle her hair. "Where's your brother? Your mom's going to be here to pick you guys up soon."

She clacked frantically on the keyboard, keeping up with the wish list of a little boy named Oliver.

"Around here somewhere."

She snapped her fingers at me. I framed up Oliver and Bones and clicked twice. "Okay, I'm gonna go find him. You stay here, all right?"

Kacey nodded and pulled a Pooh Bear border up in the program. I watched her for a minute, awed by her. So young. So smart. She had everything going for her and probably didn't even know it.

She threw a glance at me. "What?"

"Nothing," I said. "I'll be right back."

I found Alex standing in front of a display of blank journals, picking them up one by one and flipping through them.

"Whatcha doin'?" I asked, coming up behind him. He jumped and screamed.

"Jesus Christ, Wanda!" he said, putting the book back on the shelf. "You scared the hell out of me."

"Jesus Christ, Alex, don't say Jesus Christ." I pulled the book he'd been looking at off the shelf. "Since when are you interested in journals?"

"I'm not."

I flipped through it. It was lined, for writing. "Do you write?"

He shrugged. The teenager's answer to everything, from yes-or-no questions to the composition segment on their English exam. The only questions they ever answer in detail are "What do you want from McDonald's?" and "What kind of car do you want when you turn sixteen?"

I raised my eyebrows at him. "What do you write?"

He shrugged again. "I don't know."

I thunked him on the head with the book. "Yes, you do. Look, I swear, I won't make fun."

He glanced at me through the bangs he insisted on not cutting. A second later he mumbled, "Short stories, mostly."

I nodded, tucking the journal under my arm and heading to the counter. He followed behind me.

"What are you doing?" he whispered harshly.

"I like the journal. I need a journal. I'm buying it for me," I hissed back.

As soon as it was purchased, I thrust the bag at him, hitting him in the gut with it and getting in return a soft but satisfying "Ooomph!"

"I thought you said this was for you."

"It is. We haven't done anything with the puppet show yet. I need a play."

"Oh, man." Obligatory protest requirement met, he accepted the book from me and followed me toward the Station. "You're gonna make me write a stupid puppet play?"

I shrugged. "It's up to you whether it's stupid or not." I pulled out the chair next to Kacey at the desk. "Now sit down and eat your burger."

꩜

Things were winding down at the Santa Station, about fifteen minutes to closing, when I sent Anne Marie home to study for her history test the next day. There were only a few customers in the store, and not one kid, as far as I saw. Bones had left his Santa hat, wig, and coat in a lump on his Santa throne while he went off to visit the men's room, grumbling about how even legends and myths needed to take a whiz every now and again. So I was alone, fiddling around with the computer, when I heard Walter's voice behind me.

"Wanda?"

I looked up and saw him peering down at me from the other side of my desk. He was wearing a gray coat over a gray suit and a bright red tie. He looked good, and he looked like he smelled good. I wondered if there was a way I could get close enough to smell him without breaking my rules of reinvention, and my heart started hammering at the thought of what I'd do if I got that close.

Crap. This wasn't going to be good, but there was no escape. I smoothed out my elf tunic, tried to scrape up whatever fledgling remnants of confidence my psyche could muster, and plastered on a smile. "Hey. You."

Boom. Boom. Boom. My heart was hammering at full tilt. I wondered if he could see it pounding through the tunic. I was glad I'd put the kibosh on the whole elf ear thing. At least I wouldn't discover later that I'd had an entire conversation with Walter with an errant lobe sitting on my shoulder.

"So," I said, "what are you doing here?"

He held up some Osgiliath's bags. "Just a little Christmas shopping."

"Oh. Well. Good."

Our eyes locked. I could see the questions on his face. *Why did you run out? Why haven't you called? Didn't you know I was worried? Can't you see that I care?* He didn't say any of that, though. He only smiled that Jimmy Stewart smile and nodded toward my costume.

"I like your new look."

"Yeah, well, you know . . ." I cringed at my rambling and

attempted to redeem myself by resting my elbow on the desk and my chin on my hand, the way I'd seen a thousand cool supermodels do in magazines. Of course, since I was staring at Walter, my elbow missed the desk by a full inch and my forehead came cracking down on the computer keyboard.

Take me now, God, I thought. *Lightning bolt, aneurysm, alien abduction. Be creative. I'll be waiting.*

Walter was at my side in a second, kneeling before me, his hands on my shoulders. "Are you okay?"

"I'm fine," I said, slapping on a tight smile. "Great. Never better."

He reached up to touch my head where it had collided with the keyboard. I instinctively pushed his hand away.

"Oh, let me look, you big baby," he whispered. He smoothed my hair away from my face and inspected my forehead. His face was so close to mine that I could smell his aftershave. I was right. He did smell good.

Boom. Boom. Boom.

He smiled and moved back, smoothing my hair again before pulling his hand away. "I think you'll survive."

I stuck my tongue out at him and made a face. "Told ya."

He stood up and grabbed my hand to help me up. I looked around desperately to see if any kids had suddenly materialized to save me from myself. They hadn't.

"Is this your new gig?" He looked around, a soft smile on his lips as he checked out the Station. "Looks like fun."

"Yeah," I said, crossing my arms over my chest. "Yeah. I . . . I own it. Actually."

Walter smiled. "You own it? No kidding. Really?"

"No kidding, really. Bought it with Edgar Dowd's cash, as a matter of fact."

He smiled. "I'm glad you put it to good use."

There was an awkward silence. *Still waiting on that light-ning bolt, God. Tick-tock.*

"So," Walter said after a bit, "do you still see Elizabeth?"

I nodded, my eyebrows knitting. "Yeah. Don't you?"

He shrugged. "Not recently."

"Why not?" I laughed. "Did Jack finally drop that stupid lawsuit?"

Walter didn't say anything. I felt my chin drop.

"Jack dropped the lawsuit? Are you kidding?"

Walter hesitated, then gave me a careful smile. "I actually can't say. Attorney-client privilege and all. But . . . if you and Elizabeth are close . . ."

I nodded. "Yeah, we've gotten close."

"Well, then maybe you could ask her about it."

"Okay," I said. "I will."

He nodded. Another awkward silence. I glanced at the books surrounding us and had a brief and unsettling vision of what I'd do there if Walter and I were really alone. When I looked back, Walter was still looking at me. I smiled. "Well, it's about time for me to close up shop."

Walter put his hand on my arm, pulled me over, and kissed me on the cheek. "It was good to see you again, Wanda."

There were a million appropriate responses to that. I could have said, "Nice to see you." Or "Yeah, it was great, let's get coffee sometime." I could have even told him about the stickies on my wall and how I'd vowed to avoid him until I'd cleared them all away, until I'd done something meaningful and made myself worthy.

Instead, I said nothing. Walter's lips tightened and he gave a stiff smile and he walked away not having the slightest idea that my heart was still boom-boom-booming as I watched him go.

9

Chattanooga is a two-hour drive from Hastings. In mid-December, it's a gray drive, mostly highway through back country and farmland. It gave me lots of time to think about turning around and going back, crumpling up the *Talk to Molly* note and throwing it away, and who would ever know the difference?

Unfortunately, I would. That kept me going, because if I didn't face Molly again, then I wouldn't move forward, and if I didn't move forward, then I would never see Walter again.

And that was not an option.

Molly's house was at the end of a cul-de-sac. It was white. Had a picket fence. A picture so perfect it almost seemed a shame for me to bring myself into it. I pulled my car up in front of a house two doors away and got out, heading down the sidewalk toward Molly's new life. There were two cars in the driveway. It occurred to me she might have gotten married. Her last name was still Zane in the phone book, but many women did that these days. I glanced around the property. There was no sign of kids. As I walked up to the front door, I stepped around two signs of a very big dog, and I remembered Molly once saying something about wanting a dog.

I rang the doorbell and waited. There was no answer. I stepped back. Although it would have made sense to call first, I hadn't, just assuming she'd be home waiting for me to make my grand entrance back into her life. I turned around and scanned the quiet neighborhood, since the evidence suggested she was probably out walking the dog. I situated myself on the front porch and waited, hugging my knees to my chest to conserve my body heat.

I stared out at the neighborhood and imagined what Molly would look like now. Her face would be full and flush. Her hair would still be long and red. Her dog would be a Lab. Her husband would be a doctor.

And there would be no residual scars, physical or mental, from the time that my ex-husband busted her face in. Hey, if you're gonna fool yourself, fool yourself big.

My heart rate quickened as I thought about what I'd brought back into her life. I wish I'd used the drive to plan something to say when I finally saw her, instead of distracting myself with my Billy Joel CDs. I figured I'd just wing it, come out with a quick apology, and be on my way back to Hastings with one less sticky note on my mind. But what do you say to someone after you dig a big ditch through their road to recovery? How do you make up for that? *Hey, Molly, I knitted you a sweater. Goes with your eyes. All's forgiven about that time I fucked up your life, right? Greeeeaaaaaaat.*

Down the road, two women were hand in hand, walking a

dog. One of them was tall with long blonde hair. The other had short red hair. Real short. And she looked about thirty pounds lighter than the Molly I'd known. I squinted and stepped forward.

Oh my God, I thought. *I turned Molly into a lesbian.*

Molly and her girlfriend let the dog off his leash, and he came bounding toward me. Molly paused for a moment and slowed her pace as she noticed me standing on their front stoop, then hurried after the dog. The dog was a huge Great Dane and possibly the most laid-back animal I'd ever seen. He gave me a quick sniff and circled me once, seeming to approve my existence in his space. Then he walked over to lift his leg on the fence. I looked at him.

"What, they didn't just take you out for that?"

He threw a glance at me, and I swear he shrugged.

"Wanda?" Molly stood about five feet from me, staring. The blonde was another ten feet back, not looking as approving of my existence in her space as the dog had been.

"Molly. Hi."

After a moment, she smiled. I saw tears form in her eyes. She stepped forward and gave me a hug.

"It's good to see you," she said. She sounded like she meant it. That had to be good, right?

I hugged her back and then took a step toward the blonde, holding my hand out to her. "Hi. I'm Wanda. I'm not a lesbian."

It wasn't graceful, but it got the point across. The blonde smiled and shook my hand.

Greta and Molly had decorated their home country-kitchen style. I'd never seen so many knickknacks in my life. Shelves of rag dolls, little straw hausfraus, and ceramic vegetables lined the walls.

"Wow," I said, looking around. "This place must be hell to dust."

Molly smiled and placed a tray with a pitcher of iced tea and two glasses on the kitchen table. Greta came over and patted me warmly on the shoulder. "It's nice meeting you, Wanda. I've heard a great deal about you."

I smiled. "Nice meeting you, too."

She kissed Molly on the cheek. "I'm gonna give you girls some time to catch up." She put her hand on Molly's arm and gave a gentle squeeze. "I'll just be in the living room if you need me." And she left.

Molly filled our glasses and sat down.

"Greta, huh?" I said, nodding my head in the direction of the blonde's departure and giving Molly a grin. "I didn't know you had it in you."

She smiled, and I saw a faint blush on her cheeks. "So tell me about yourself," she said, leaning back in her seat. "How have you been?"

"Good," I said. "I left Channel 8."

"That's good," she said softly. "I don't think that place was good for you."

"Yeah. I think you're right."

There was a moment of silence in which a big white elephant named George sat down in the middle of the table. There was only one way to get rid of him, so I did it.

"I tracked you down because I needed to talk to you," I said. "I needed to tell you that I'm really sorry. About what happened." Silence. I took a sip of my tea and then elaborated unnecessarily. "With George."

Poof. Elephant gone.

"You shouldn't be," she said. "I let him drag you out of the house. I should have called the police. I should have done something."

It had never occurred to me for a second that she might not hate and resent me, that she might feel bad for not having done enough for me. Just goes to show, a little self-absorption goes a long way.

"No, no, it wasn't your fault at all." I felt the emotion catch in my throat. "That's just . . . crazy."

"I abandoned you to him." Her voice was small and tight. "You needed help, and I ran away."

"You had just gotten your life back together. I brought all that crap right to your doorstep."

"I was so scared," she said, and looked up at me as the tears spilled over her cheeks. "I'm so sorry."

"No." I grabbed her hand and gave it a squeeze, watching as her face blurred through my own tears. "*I'm* sorry."

Greta appeared out of nowhere, dropping a box of tissues on the table, handing each of us a smile, then wordlessly retreating back to the living room. I grabbed a tissue and wiped my face.

"You know, it's not my style, but I can kind of see where you're coming from," I said, nodding in Greta's direction. "There isn't a man in the world that would ever do that."

Molly laughed. "Yeah, she's great. I don't know what I'd do without her."

We sat back, wiping our eyes, blowing our noses, and staring at the walls full of knickknacks. Then I broke the silence. "So you mean all this time, you really thought that was all your fault?"

Molly nodded, and she teared up again. "I haven't forgiven myself. I should have stayed. I shouldn't have let him take you away. I should have called the police. I should have pressed charges." She heaved a staggered sigh. "He could have killed you."

I smiled. "But he didn't."

She smiled back. "That's right. He didn't."

We clinked our iced-tea glasses together and drank, and I pretended that George wasn't still out there, somewhere, probably still looking to kill me. The world could sometimes be a much better place when you didn't acknowledge reality.

"I'm going to count backwards from three," the soft voice hummed. "When I get to one, you will open your eyes, and you will feel rested and relaxed, and you will know the name of the song you've been hearing. Three . . . two . . . one."

I opened my eyes. The room was darkened, and the smell of incense was cutting a swath through my sinuses. The hypnotist, a small, wiry woman named Grace, leaned into my line of vision. "How do you feel?"

"Rested. Relaxed."

Grace smiled a toothy, gapped smile. She was a woman in

her fifties who operated out of her basement. When she took me down there, I half expected her to offer me a good deal on some pot. Looking at her, I still wouldn't have been surprised if she had a stash in a back room.

"Can you identify the song?" Grace asked. I leaned back against the sofa and rubbed my eyes. I listened. The music floated in. The crescendo built. I hummed along. It disappeared.

"No. Can you?"

She leaned forward. "Hum it again?"

I hummed it again. She shook her head. "No. Sounds familiar, though."

"Yeah," I said. "That's my problem." I pulled out my checkbook.

"Hey, Grace," I said as I scribbled away eighty-five dollars I'd never get back. "How did you know you wanted to be a hypnotherapist?"

She smiled. "The aliens told me."

I raised an eyebrow at her. This was what you got for picking someone at random from the yellow pages.

"Don't suppose those aliens can tell you what my song is, do you?"

She laughed. "No. They can't read minds."

"Okay, thanks so much for your time," I said, handing her the check. "And may the force be with you."

෧෨

"I am so excited!" Elizabeth placed two glasses of milk on the table and grabbed a warm chocolate chip cookie off the plate.

Her face was bright and her eyes were lively. "The radio station is so cool. I only have to work between nine and three, and I have my own office."

I dunked a cookie into the milk. "I feel kinda guilty eating the good stuff after the kids are in bed."

"Get over it," she said, stuffing a chunk of cookie in her mouth. "That's the first thing you have to learn before you become a mom, or you'll waste easily three or four years just beating yourself up over stupid shit."

I nodded and dunked the cookie again. "Good advice, Dr. Mackey."

"I'm not a doctor." She dunked, then smiled. "Matt, my producer, wanted to call the show *Dr. Liz*. He was really surprised when I told him I wasn't a doctor."

"Really?"

"Yeah," she said, smiling as she popped a bit of cookie into her mouth. "He said I was so smart that it never occurred to him that I wasn't a doctor. Isn't that sweet?"

"Oh, man," I said, shaking my head.

"What?"

I laughed. "Nothing. I just can't help but notice the special smile when you mentioned Matt. Is there something you're not telling me?"

Elizabeth flushed. "No. Not yet." She grinned and took another bite of her cookie. "But he's been sending . . . I don't know . . . vibes."

"Beware the vibe," I said. "Whatever happened to that 'I'd rather be alone forever' crap you were trying to feed me?"

Elizabeth sighed. "Sometimes saying 'never' or 'forever' makes it easier to get through the day. And, I mean, it's not like Matt and I are dating. It's just that I'm . . . open to possibilities."

"I don't know," I said. "I'm not sure it's a great idea to open up your possibilities to your boss."

She chewed thoughtfully for a moment, then shook her head and grinned. "Just because something's not a great idea doesn't mean you shouldn't do it."

I held up my glass of milk. "Preaching to the choir, sister."

On that, we clinked our glasses and drank.

10

That weekend, the kids went with Jack to visit his mother, and Elizabeth went to Atlanta to see her sister. I scheduled Anne Marie, Bones, and various hired elves to run the Santa Station and had an entire weekend to myself.

The first thing I did was head to the grocery store and buy as much junk as I wanted. Around the kids, I was trying to help Elizabeth set a good example, so I'd been up to my ears in apples and graham crackers and orange juice. Now that they were gone, it was all Doritos and Coke, pudding and M&M's. I was going to be sick as a dog and wearing sweatpants all the next week, but it would be worth it.

And, for old times' sake, I got a bottle of my old friend, Albert.

Friday afternoon and evening, I watched cable television. There was a twelve-hour *Trading Spaces* marathon, and about five hours in, I started to wallow. I was thirty-two years old, eating Doritos on a sofa that wasn't mine, and watching neighbors decorate each other's homes on a television that wasn't mine. The only neighbor I'd ever known in my entire adult life was Elizabeth, and I couldn't even trade spaces with her because I was living in her damn house.

The realization that I was a spinster freeloader crying over a home design show took me to a new low. This was even worse than the Lifetime movie thing. I looked over to my lonely bottle of Albert, sitting untouched in a brown paper bag on the coffee table.

Two hours later I was still watching *Trading Spaces*, with a Scotch flush on my cheeks now, and the pathetic feeling of being a permanent resident in Loserville had cemented into firm, unyielding blocks around my ankles.

I slept on the sofa, waking up when the first light of morning infused a pale glow into the drapes. My head hurt, my stomach was queasy, and the realization hit me that I was way too old for this shit. I took the Doritos, the M&M's, and Albert, put them all in a big trash bag, and walked it out to the curb, returning to retrieve Albert at the last minute. Dad had been right about some days requiring Scotch. I stuffed the bottle into the back of Elizabeth's liquor cabinet, knowing that someday I'd probably be grateful I did.

Even with the trash on the corner and an orange digesting nicely in my stomach, I didn't feel better. Restless, I grabbed the keys to my car and headed out to Wal-Mart, where I bought a pair of running shoes, blue shiny nylon running pants with stripes down the sides, a T-shirt with that obnoxious Nike "Just Do It" slogan on the front. If it wasn't for my love handles and some serious thigh jiggle, someone might even have taken me for the athletic type.

It was still fairly early in the morning when I headed out for my run. I ran to the end of the driveway and tripped over the trash bag while trying to pull off the tag that I'd left on the neck of my T-shirt. It wasn't a sterling start.

It's also important to note that just because pants are shiny and nylon and have running stripes on them, it doesn't necessarily make them running pants. Or maybe it was that my wearing shiny nylon pants with running stripes didn't necessarily make me a runner. At any rate, I hadn't made it to the end of the street before I decided that maybe power walking was more my style.

I power walked through Elizabeth's neighborhood, trying not to look like a geek with my elbows kicking and my legs snapping. The air was just cold enough to be sharp on my lungs, but not so cold that a little movement couldn't keep me comfortable. I zipped through Such-and-Such Lane and Cute-Suburban-Home Way and marveled at how many wind socks these people seemed to need.

I was about halfway around So-Cute-You-Could-Just-Throw-Up Circle when I saw it. Like all the other lawns, it was perfectly manicured and had about a foot of chilled morning mist hovering above its surface. What was different on this one was the For Sale sign. I slowed down and walked up the driveway to the single-car garage and picked out a sheet from the plastic box hanging on the Realtor's sign.

Hardwood Floors.

Fireplace.

Open Floor Plan.

I walked up to the window and pressed my nose against it, trying to see inside through the slats in the blinds. It was empty, but that was about all I could tell, except that the hardwood floors looked shiny and full of promise. I folded the Realtor's sheet into eighths, stuffed it in my pants pocket, and power walked back to Elizabeth's house, my mind whirling with possibilities and pipe dreams.

A half hour later I was boiling water for instant oatmeal when the phone rang. I glanced at it and let it ring, figuring Elizabeth's answering machine would take a more reliable message than I would. The machine clicked, Elizabeth did her "Leave a message at the beep" routine, and then Walter's voice came through the line.

"Elizabeth? This is Walter Briggs. I'm looking for Wanda. I don't know where she is, and I need to talk—"

"Hey, Walter," I said, my breath almost as choppy as when I was running. My heart had started boom-boom-booming at the sound of his voice, and I had practically cracked my kneecap lunging for the phone. "What's up?"

"Wanda?" His voice sounded tense. "I'm glad you're there."

"Yeah," I said, coiling the cord in my hands, almost cutting off the circulation. "What's going on?"

He paused for a moment. "I need you to meet me at Hastings General," he said. "I think we've found your ex-husband."

Walter was waiting in front of the hospital entrance when I got there. He looked so young, standing out in the cold with his hands tucked in the front pockets of his jeans, his Harvard sweatshirt ruffling a bit in the breeze. He took a step toward me when he saw me coming.

"Hey," he said with a concerned smile. "How are you?"

"Peachy. What's up?" I asked him, a little annoyed at the "I'd rather tell you in person" bit he'd given me on the phone.

"Let's go inside." He put his hand on my elbow and guided me through the automatic doors toward the hospital lobby.

"Walter," I said, running my hands over my arms, "are you trying to freak me out? Because if you are, you're doing a really super job."

Walter sat me down in a row of seats by the registration desk, taking a seat next to me. His face was taut, his eyes locked on mine. I tried to glean some clues from his expression, but all I got was that there was news and it was bad.

"Remember my friend the private investigator who was looking for your ex?"

I nodded, my mind leaping from scenario to scenario, imagining what George had done to land himself in Hastings General. I saw fleeting images of bar brawls, resisting arrests, drunken car accidents. I felt Walter's hand covering mine, and I entwined my fingers tightly in his.

"We think we may have found him. Here, in town." I had images of him in my apartment, destroying my things. Scaring or hurting my landlady, Mrs. Forini. Harassing my neighbors. I heard Walter say something, but it was lost in the static in my head.

Walter leaned his face down into my line of vision. "Did you hear me? We need you to identify the body."

"The body?" I said, my heart clenched as my mind snapped to Mrs. Forini. But she has family here. They wouldn't need me to identify . . .

Oh. A hush fell over my world. I replayed Walter's words in my mind, finally accepting on a conscious level what I'd known the moment I heard his voice on the phone but hadn't yet been ready to believe.

George was dead.

"Okay," I said, standing up. "Okay."

Walter put his hand on my shoulder. "Are you sure you're ready to do this? Do you need a moment to—?"

"To what?" I asked. "To prepare myself? How exactly would I do that?"

He nodded and guided me to the nurses' desk, asking for directions to the morgue, explaining to the woman at the desk who I was, handling the whole situation so that I didn't have to say a word.

As we whirled through the hospital, I got the story from Walter. His friend had picked up George's scent in Kansas but lost him in Mississippi. A few days earlier one of his police buddies had mentioned arresting a guy from Alaska. He checked up on it and found that one George Lewis had been brought in on a drunk-and-disorderly and had been released to the Randall P. McKay Shelter for Men. When Walter's buddy went there to follow up, he was told that George Lewis had died in his sleep the night before.

Now it was up to me to determine if the dead George Lewis was my George Lewis.

An elevator ride and one long, narrow hallway later, the morgue attendant was leading us to a wall of metallic drawers, pulling one out and folding the sheet down to reveal George's face. It's a funeral home cliché, the whole "He looked so much like himself" thing people say about the dead. George still had the scar above his left eye that he'd gotten in a knife fight before I met him, and the birthmark on his chin was exactly where it used to be. But he looked nothing like George. He looked wooden, and cold, and peaceful. George had never seen a peaceful day in his life, and he certainly hadn't earned one in death.

The attendant gave an uncomfortable cough, then, "Is this your husband, ma'am?"

I nodded. "Ex-husband. Yes."

"Is there anyone else we should notify?"

I shook my head. George had lost contact with his family before I'd met him. I didn't even know where they were. "I'm it."

Walter touched my elbow. "Do you want to sit down?"

"Can I go outside?" I asked. My voice sounded high and tight like a little girl's. My limbs felt like they were made of foam. "Can you just get me outside?"

Walter nodded, his hand on my elbow as he led me through the hospital hallways. The first outside door we found led to a central atrium, where they'd planted a garden with a statue of the Virgin Mary in the middle. Stone benches circled around her like subjects kneeling before a queen.

But it was all just a bunch of dead stone.

Walter led me to one of the benches and sat me down. He sat next to me as I stared at the Virgin. He was still and silent, waiting for me to speak first, another statue in the midst of a garden made for mourning.

Snippets of memories wafted through my head like faint aromas in an attic. George bouncing at Pappy's, buying me drinks when I was still underage. Zipping down the highway on the back of his motorcycle, my arms wrapped around his strong chest, feeling like nothing could touch us. The hate and anger in his eyes that I couldn't understand. The fury I felt when he hurt Molly. How I separated from myself when he kept me captive that weekend, watching him terrorizing me from a distance, only a taut string of fear keeping me shackled to myself.

How he had no right. How he had no fucking right.

How he was dead.

"I thought I'd be happy," I said finally, surprised by the sound of my voice as the words came out on their own. I stared at the Virgin, speaking as much to her as to Walter. "I've been praying for this for a long time. I know it's terrible, but it's true. And now here I am, and he's finally gone, and I'm not even relieved. I'm sad, actually."

"That's understandable," Walter said calmly, always the voice of reason. "I'm sure you loved him. Once."

"I should hate him," I said, my eyes drifting back to the Virgin. "I should be happy he's finally gone."

I paused, but I didn't know what I was waiting for. The music maybe. Now would be a good time for the music to make sense. Now would be a good time for anything to make sense. But, of course, nothing did. Not George, not Walter, not the Virgin in her garden of stone.

"He loved me." I nearly choked on the words as I said them. "He may have been a sick bastard and a bad guy, but he loved me, and he was the only one who did. I know it sounds crazy . . ."

"No," Walter said quietly, "it doesn't."

"And instead of being relieved that I don't have to be afraid of him anymore, I feel like the last person who will ever love me is just . . . gone."

Walter put his arm around my shoulders, pulling me tight against him. I collapsed onto him, sobbing under the weight of George's life and death. Walter held me, rocking me back and forth, kissing my hair, and whispering quietly, "He won't be the last one."

We sat like that for a while, until I recovered enough to realize I was getting cold out there in my shiny nylon running pants and T-shirt. Walter pulled off his sweatshirt, revealing a worn-out Rolling Stones '86 World Tour T-shirt underneath. I smiled. He pulled the sweatshirt over my head and put his arm around my waist, guiding me silently through the halls of Hastings General until we were in the parking lot.

I started to take off the sweatshirt when we got to my car, but Walter put his hand out to stop me.

"Keep it." He smiled. "I'll get it later."

I nodded and unlocked my car door but turned back to Walter before opening it.

"Thank you," I said.

He shrugged. "I'm glad you didn't have to do this alone."

"No," I said. "I mean for everything. I don't make it easy for people to . . . help me." I swallowed. "To care about me. I know that."

He smiled. "It's okay."

"And I'm sorry," I said. He nodded, although I could tell he wanted to ask what I was sorry for. Sorry I'd kissed him? Sorry I'd slept with him? Sorry I'd left him? All of the above? I reached over and grabbed his hand. "Can you do something for me?"

I felt his fingers tighten around mine. "Anything."

"Don't give up on me," I said. I could feel my eyes filling again, and I blinked the tears away. Stupid, mushy, crying fool.

Walter pulled me into his arms and hugged me, kissing the top of my head and breathing a little lightness back into me. "I wasn't planning on it."

I pulled away and got in my car and drove back to Elizabeth's, taking a hit off the smell of Walter's sweatshirt every now and again to keep me going.

෧෨

Sunday morning I woke up on Elizabeth's sofa. I'd been unable to go to sleep the night before and had crawled down to the living room and switched on a documentary channel. I fell asleep to sharks and woke up to baboon asses. It wasn't pretty.

I headed out to steal some empty cardboard boxes from the Dumpster behind the grocery store. An hour later I had one box on my shoulder and another under my arm as I headed up the steps to my old second-floor apartment. Before putting my key in the lock, I turned and looked out toward the city of Hastings, shielded behind a veil of flour, and remembered standing there with Walter after that first kiss, pondering silently on the existence of purity. I laughed a little, amazed at how sometimes a few weeks could seem like a lifetime.

I pushed the door open and stepped in, my foot sliding a bit as it made contact with an envelope. It was a standard business envelope, with "Wanda" scrawled in George's handwriting on the front. Judging by the scuffs on it, he had taken some time shoving it under the rubber runners that weatherproofed my front door. As I bent down to pick it up, I heard a familiar voice behind me.

"That's one hell of an ass, cupcake." I stood up and turned to see Manny the Mailman. "You can't be sticking out an ass like that just anywhere. You might give some poor guy a heart attack."

"Hey, Manny," I said. "What are you doing here? There's no mail on Sundays."

"Ah, there was a weird guy hanging around here a week back. Mrs. Forini called the cops, but he left before they got here. I been checking up for her. She was pretty freaked out." He gave me a pointed look. "So where the hell ya been, babe?"

"I had a little domestic problem," I said. "I had to get away for a while."

His face darkened. "Was it that guy?"

I gave a small smile. "Yeah. He won't be back."

"What about you?" he asked. "You back?"

I shook my head. "I'm just cleaning out the apartment. I found a place I like better."

Manny nodded. "Yeah. Well. Good for you. Glad you're

okay." He reached over and gave me a pat on the back. "Take care of yourself."

I waved after him as he bounded down the steps. When he was almost at his car, I yelled out, "Hey, Manny!"

He turned and shielded his eyes against the sun to look up at me. "What?"

"You let me know if you ever leave that wife of yours, okay?"

"Ah, you," he said, giving me a wave of dismissal and getting in his car. I dropped the envelope into one empty box and headed back into my apartment to pack up.

Later that afternoon I came out from the shower, stepping over the piles of stuff I'd kept from the old place. It wasn't much. Books and pictures, mostly. Everything else I'd donated to a women's shelter downtown. It was time for a new start, anyway.

I towel-dried my hair on the bed and stared at the remaining sticky notes on my wall.

Get a new haircut.

Go see parents.

Do something meaningful.

Identify phantom music.

Figure out what I want.

Tell Walter.

I focused on the last one and wished I hadn't vowed to take care of everything else before really talking to him. I knew I could call him, and he'd be over in a flash, holding me, making me feel better. Giving everything and demanding nothing.

Which was exactly why I had to get through the other stuff first.

I threw the towel onto the pile of laundry in the corner and tossed myself back on the bed, staring at the ceiling. Maybe I should just forget the whole thing and call him. Maybe this reinvention of self was just a big old truckload of bullshit I invented to fuel my avoidance. Well, I didn't want to avoid Walter anymore. I wanted to move on, with him if possible.

Screw the sticky notes.

Screw the goddamn sticky notes.

I sighed, grabbing the cordless phone from its base. I pulled one of the sticky notes off the wall and grabbed the phone book, letting my fingers do the walking through the Beauty Salons & Stylists section.

"I want something different," I said, tapping my feet on the bar at the bottom of the stylist's chair.

The unfortunate stylist who'd gotten me was a girl with pink hair named Anna, who tilted her head and looked at me.

"Just . . . different?" I could see the dread in her face. I imagined the last woman who'd said that to her leaving in tears, threatening to sue, seemingly unaware that hair grows back.

"Yes. I don't care what you do. Just make it different. Red, maybe. Or blonde. Short. Layered. Bobbed. I don't care. Have fun. I'm your own personal Barbie doll."

"Really?" she said, her eyes brightening.

I nodded. "Really."

Anna grinned and cracked her gum. "Cool."

$$\infty$$

"What did you do to your hair?" Elizabeth asked, dropping her bag in the hallway, too surprised by my new look to notice that she'd left the door open and that a tall, good-looking, and apparently very happy man was still standing right behind her. "It's all short. And red!"

I stepped forward and extended my hand to the man behind her.

"You must be Matt," I said. He smiled and shook my hand.

"I guess Elizabeth has mentioned me, then?" he asked, a hint of uncertainty in his voice as his eyes darted to Elizabeth, who wrapped her arms around his waist.

"This is Matt," she said. "Matt, this is Wanda."

"Nice to finally meet you," Matt said. It was a little disconcerting how much he was like a Ken doll come to life, but after checking out the smile on Elizabeth's face, I decided not to hold it against him.

"Sorry I lied about going to see my sister, Wanda," Elizabeth said, looking like a kid who'd just got caught at a nightclub when she'd told her parents she was studying at the library. "I just wasn't ready to let everyone know yet."

I waved my hand at her. "Don't worry about it. I won't say a word." I gave them both a smile, pulled the dish towel off my shoulder, and headed back into the kitchen. "I'm gonna let you say good-bye to your sister."

Two minutes later Elizabeth was in the kitchen with me, sampling my spaghetti sauce off a wooden spoon and gushing about her weekend with Matt.

"We had such a good time. He's so great." She giggled. "Oh, God. I'm giggling. Slap me, would you?"

"No," I said. I poured us each a glass of wine and leaned against the kitchen counter. "George is dead."

Elizabeth straightened up. "Oh my God, Wanda. What happened? Are you okay?"

I gave her a brief rundown of events, excluding the bit with Walter. I wasn't ready to talk about him yet. She pulled me into a hug, and I patted her shoulder and pulled away, smiling and squeezing her hand.

"It's okay. It was rough at first, but I'm okay." I turned my back to her, attending to the pasta I was cooking, not wanting my face to give away that I wasn't entirely okay just yet. "I mean, it's over, right? That's what matters. It's over."

I heard Elizabeth draw in a breath to speak, but the sounds of the kids at the front door stopped her.

"We'll talk later," she said, putting her wine down and rushing into the living room. I followed her, coming in as she knelt down to hug the kids. Jack was standing on the front stoop, careful to stay outside until invited in.

Elizabeth stood up, ruffling Alex's hair as he retreated to his room, and pulling Kacey to her. She looked up at Jack and smiled. "Hi, Jack."

Jack smiled back at her, a surprised expression on his face. "Hi, Elizabeth. How are you?"

"I'm great. And you?"

"Good," he said. "I heard the promos on the radio for your show. It sounds like it's going to be good."

She nodded. "Thanks. I'm really excited about it."

Kacey tugged at Elizabeth. "Mom, I want to show you the new chemistry kit that Grandma got me. Come on," she said, pulling Elizabeth's arm.

"I'll be right back," she said with a grin, letting Kacey lead her away. I walked over to stand by the door, where Jack watched Elizabeth bound up the steps behind their daughter.

"That's the first time I've seen her smile in . . . I don't even know how long." He ran his fingers through his hair and gave me a hopeful grin. "That radio thing must really be good for her, huh?"

"There's someone else," I said quietly. I didn't want to blow Elizabeth's secret, but it had to be said. "Don't tell the kids. She's not ready to tell them yet. I thought you should know, though."

"Oh." His smile faded briefly, then returned on a wave of determined effort. "Oh. Well, good for her. That's good. Is he a nice guy?"

"I've only met him briefly," I said, "but he seems like it, yeah."

Jack nodded. "Okay. He makes her happy, then?"

"Yeah," I said. "I think so."

He nodded again. "Okay."

There was a short silence. I tried to think about Jack and the various biddies, tried to remember that he had earned this in spades, but it didn't make me feel any better watching him standing there in the doorway while his family drifted away from him.

He clapped his hands together and faked a smile. "Well, hey, I need to go. Can you tell them I said good-bye?"

"Yeah," I said with a small smile. "I'll tell them."

He squeezed my hand briefly, then disappeared into the night. I shut the door and hollered up the steps, "Somebody better haul their butt down here and eat some spaghetti with me!"

∞

"What the hell did you do to yourself, Wanda?" Bones grumbled. "Your hair's all red. And short. You might be able to pull that off if you were black, but on a white girl . . . damn. You look like a big match."

It was early Tuesday morning, and Osgiliath's was just about to open. I swiveled around in the chair to see Bones, his skinny little neck sticking up from the padded Santa suit, the wig and cap tucked under his arm.

"Coming from a skinny black Santa Claus, I'll take that as a compliment."

Bones grunted and settled himself into his Santa throne,

picking up a small device at his feet that I hadn't seen before. "Get your ass over here."

I eyed him suspiciously, standing up but not moving. "What're you up to, Bones?"

"I'm old, child," he yelled back at me. "You take too long. I might not be alive by the time you get here."

I walked over to stand next to him, looked at the device in his hand and then back at him. "Bones, what the hell—?"

He grabbed me, and before I knew it, I was sitting in his lap.

"Bones!" I said, trying to get up. I would have never thought Bones could pack so much strength into such a small frame, but my struggling was pointless. I was going nowhere.

"Bones, let me go."

He pointed to the camera. "Now, you look into that camera and you smile nice."

I crossed my arms. "Bones, what the hell are you doing?"

"Good God but you are a difficult woman," he growled. "Just shut up and sit tight."

I relaxed, put my arm around his shoulder, and grinned to the camera. He clicked the device in his hand, and about two seconds later the flash went off. He loosened his grip, and I got up. "What is that?"

"Remote control, so Kacey tells me," he said, smiling. "Now, go print out that picture."

I walked over to the computer and looked down to see a woman I didn't recognize. She was laughing and pretty and happy as she sat on the lap of the oldest, blackest Santa Claus I'd ever seen.

"You done printing that damn thing out yet?" Bones hollered at me.

"Just a minute, you old goat," I yelled back at him. I clicked through the borders and found a book theme, then hit print twice. When it was done, I walked up and gave one to Bones, who inspected it through his bifocals. After a moment, he looked up and smiled.

"What do you want for Christmas, girl?" he asked.

I leaned over and patted him on the shoulder, speaking in a breathless, Marilyn Monroe voice. "I'd tell you, Santa, but I think it might kill you."

❧

"Hey, Wanda, what's that envelope on the counter?" Kacey asked.

I glanced up from the kitchen table where Alex was whooping my ass at chess and saw George's envelope. I'd dropped it on the counter after I came home from clearing out my apartment and hadn't touched it since. Elizabeth must have figured it was sensitive, because she'd been cleaning around it for most of the past week. I knew I'd have to deal with it some-day but had successfully procrastinated.

Until now.

"It's from my ex-husband." I turned back to the chess game. Moved my queen. "Check."

Alex scoffed. "That's not a check."

I stared at the board. He was right. Damn. I moved the queen back. I sucked at chess, but the kids loved it, so I swallowed my pride and got killed in a tournament at least once a week.

Kacey was still looking at the envelope. "You know, you're going to have to open it eventually."

I rolled my eyes and looked at her. "Can't you just be twelve for a few minutes? Sit on the sofa and play Barbies?"

Her face contorted into an expression of disgust. "(A) Twelve-year-olds don't play with Barbies, and (B) do you know that if a real woman had Barbie's proportions, she'd have to carry her kidneys in her—?"

I held up my hand. "Oh my God, you have been hanging out with me too long."

I moved my bishop. No check, but it was a legal move.

"Do you want me to open it for you?" Kacey asked quietly, eyeing the envelope with curiosity. I sighed. It's possible that whatever was in there might not be appropriate for Kacey to see. It could be a nasty letter. It could be a small bomb.

Okay, George wasn't that smart. But it could be a nasty letter.

It made a tiny tinkling sound when it moved, though, which letters didn't tend to do. And if Kacey opened it, that meant I wouldn't have to touch it.

"All right. Go ahead."

Alex took my bishop with his rook. "Checkmate."

"What?" I stared at the board. "Where?"

Alex pointed to his rook, my king, and then his knight. I was cornered.

Checkmate.

"Shit." I thunked my hand on the table. "I mean, goshdarnit."

Alex leaned forward. "I don't know why you do that. Mom curses all the time."

I rolled my eyes at him. "She tries to keep a lid on it in front of you. And besides, I've got enough bad karma without corrupting a minor."

"It's a necklace."

I looked up. Kacey was holding up a silver chain with a medallion hanging from it. I stood up and walked over to her. She was holding her hand out so I could get a closer look. I still wasn't prepared to touch it.

"St. Erasmus," I said, reading the inscription curving around the edge.

St. *Erasmus?*

Either the world is full of coincidences or there's no such thing as coincidence.

"You okay, Wanda?" Kacey asked. My hand was shaking. I glanced at the envelope.

"Is that all that was in there?"

Kacey nodded. "Do you want to put it on?"

Did I want to put it on? Did I want to wear a saint medal from my rotten bastard of a dead ex-husband?

I shook my head. "Not now. Could you put it back in the envelope for me, please?"

Kacey stuffed it back in and closed the envelope. Alex was setting up the chessboard again. Kacey squealed and jumped into my seat. "I take winner! I take winner!"

I picked up the envelope by its edge, trying not to touch any more of it than I had to.

"Hey, kids. Tell your mom I had to run out for a bit, okay?"

They both grunted at me, attention fully on the chess-board. I headed out the back door, tossed the envelope into the back of my car, and drove straight for St. Benedict's.

11

Forgive me, Father, but I'm still not Catholic."

It was hard coming up with clever lines all the time. The drive from Elizabeth's to St. Benedict's took twenty minutes, and that was the best I could come up with. It still got a chuckle out of Father Gregory, though, so it was worth it.

"Wanda, how are you? Done anything meaningful yet?"

I shrugged, which probably wasn't terribly effective through the grate. *Do something meaningful* was still on my wall, as were *Identify phantom music* and *Tell Walter* and *Go see parents* and *Figure out what I want*. But I had made some small gains.

"I got a haircut."

"Well, that's a start."

"My ex-husband is dead, Father Gregory."

There was a long silence. I sat back and stared at the cathedral ceiling. It was a beautiful mix of ivory shadows, and I couldn't imagine how in the world they kept it so sparkling clean.

"I'm sorry for your loss."

"Don't be. I wished him dead, Father. I wished him dead a million times. And now I feel . . . hollow. I'm not relieved, but I'm not sad. I'm just . . . I'm numb. I don't feel anything. Shouldn't I be feeling . . . something?"

"Have you forgiven him?"

I shook my head. "Sure."

"Would you like to say a prayer for his soul?"

"Hell, no." I could hear that one bounce off the confessional, right on up to God. I put my face in my hands. "Is there a patron saint for someone who can't keep her stupid mouth shut?"

He laughed softly. "I'll have to research that one for you."

There was more silence. It was Sunday afternoon, and there would likely be people waiting. But I didn't want to rush. I still hadn't gotten to the point yet.

I heard the bench creak as he shifted his weight. "I tell you what. Go home. Take some time to think. Try to find forgiveness in your heart for your ex-husband. Then come back, and we'll talk about it a little more."

I felt tears sting my eyes. "What if I can't forgive him?"

"You can always forgive. It's not a feat, it's a choice."

"Oh, for crying out loud, Father, can't you cut me some slack? Just once? Sake of variety?"

"If you wanted slack, you wouldn't have come here."

I sighed. *Fine.* I swiped at my face. "Hey, Father Gregory?"

"Yes?"

"Remember when you told me to buy the St. Erasmus medal?"

"Yes."

I inhaled. "He got me one."

"What?"

I spoke louder. "He got me one. Before he died. The bastard shoved it under the door of my apartment."

Silence. I could hear him breathing. But he didn't say anything.

"Father Gregory, how could he have known that? I mean, I'm not Catholic. How could he have known?"

He sighed, and I heard the bench creak again as he shifted. "Sometimes people just know things."

"So, what?" I said, exasperated. "So he just turned psychic? Just like that, right before he croaked?"

"I don't believe in psychic ability," Father Gregory said. "I believe in God."

I chewed on that one. "That doesn't help me, because I don't know what to believe."

Father Gregory gave a light chuckle. "Sometimes, Wanda, that's exactly the point."

I made my excuses and got out. The confessional seemed smaller than usual. I needed some air. I walked out into the parking lot, not sure what I was going to do next. I got into my car, looked at the envelope on the backseat containing St. Erasmus, patron saint of navigators.

"Fine," I said to St. Erasmus, starting up the car. "I'm gonna drive. You tell me where to go. If it's good, I won't flush you down the toilet."

∽

Molly wasn't home when I got there, so I sat down in the driveway next to the back gate. The Great Dane, who was named Putter after Greta's love of golf, was lying down in the backyard. When he saw me, he got up, lumbered over, and plopped himself down, resting against the gate. Had to admit, the company was nice.

The St. Erasmus medal was still in the car. I hadn't touched it after throwing it onto the backseat. It enraged me, this idea that George bought me a Catholic symbol, like he was using me to get a last-ditch shot at heaven.

Even more infuriating was that it was one I'd wanted. How could he have known? Or did he not know, and it was just some elaborate joke God had cooked up to get at me for flirting with priests in the confessional?

"Do you think the world just converges sometimes, Putter?" I said, sticking my fingers through the gate and scratching behind one tremendous ear. "Do you think that sometimes stuff just happens a certain way because it's supposed to? Do you believe in coincidence?"

His body heaved in a contented dog sigh. "I don't know," he said. "I'm just a dog."

Molly and Greta pulled up about a half hour after I got there. I helped them carry groceries into the house. They made me iced tea.

"So . . . he's dead?" Molly was having trouble getting used to the thought. Maybe she was jealous. Her ex was in jail, but he was still alive. And he had a parole hearing every two years.

"Yeah," I said. "I identified him. Looked pretty dead to me."

Molly nodded. She looked like she was in about as much shock as I'd been. Maybe she'd wished him dead, too. Even when someone was a rotten bastard, and even when you were in touch with reality, it was still hard not to feel a little guilt when he dropped dead.

"The thing is," I went on, "I don't feel anything. I did at first. I was a mess. It was an intense five minutes. Then, after that, it's like . . . nothing."

I looked up at Molly. She was staring at her hands. Greta had tears in her eyes. She didn't even know me or George. It must be hard to get up in the morning when you're that empathetic.

"I loved him once," I continued, a little quieter. "He was a total shit, but for a long time, I loved him. Am I a horrible person for not feeling anything now that he's dead?"

"No." Greta's voice was low and choppy. "You have feelings. You're just shut down. They'll come, in time."

I nodded. "How long, do you think? Because I'd really like to . . . you know . . . move on." I made a sailing upward motion with my hands. "I don't want him to have power over me . . . still. I need . . ." I sighed and rolled my eyes, knowing I was going to sound like Father Gregory. But maybe that wasn't such a bad thing. "I think I need to find it in my heart to forgive him."

Molly nodded emphatically. "I know what you mean. But how can you?"

"I don't know. I mean, how do you forgive something like that? Have you forgiven your ex-husband?"

Molly paused, looking down at her hands, which were resting on her abdomen. After a moment, she shook her head.

"And how many years has it been?"

"Five."

"Jesus!" I said, throwing my hands up in the air. "I don't have five years to burn on this man."

Greta stood up. "I have an idea."

∽

The campground was almost empty. Mid-December was not a big camping time in Tennessee. We emptied out Molly's SUV of everything we'd brought with us. A tent, three sleeping bags, pillows, wood, a little food including the necessary s'mores ingredients, Putter, and two boxes.

One Molly's, one mine.

Molly and I got the tent set up under Putter's relaxed supervision while Greta made the fire. Greta had grown up in the great wilds of Montana, which made her our unofficial camp headmistress. By the time we'd thrown the sleeping bags inside the tent, the chill and gray of dusk were being held at bay by a tremendous bonfire.

I settled into the flannel shirt and jeans I'd bought when we hit the Wal-Mart. I put on the thick socks and the carpenter's boots and felt one with nature, style-wise, anyway. If any form of wildlife came near me, I'd scream and hide behind Putter, but that was a bridge I'd cross when it came scurrying toward me.

Greta pulled out what looked like a big batch of small twigs and lit them at the edge of the fire. Molly and I sat down on some tremendous logs that encircled the fire pit, with Putter inserting himself between us at our feet.

I leaned over toward Molly as I watched Greta waving the smoldering twigs in the air, apparently saying some sort of prayer, although I couldn't hear the words between the crackling of the fire and Putter's awe-inspiring snore. "What is she doing?"

Molly smiled, watching Greta with an expression of pride. "She's burning sage. It's supposed to clear the energy."

"Clear the energy?"

"Yeah. It's called smudging. It's a Native American thing."

"Is she Native American?" I asked. Tall. Skinny. Blonde. She looked Swedish to me.

"No, but you don't have to be Native to smudge. You just have to believe."

Greta moved to the other side of the fire. We could barely see her through the flames.

"What's she doing now?"

"She's saying a prayer to the east, west, north, and south. Then all the negativity will be gone, and we can continue."

"No offense," I said, reaching into our food bag and pulling out a handful of Cool Ranch Doritos, "but it seems kinda weird to me."

Molly laughed, her freckled face glowing in the light of the fire. "Yeah, I thought so, too, when she did it in every room of the house. But I'll tell ya, I haven't had any negative-energy problems."

I shrugged. I had to grant Molly that. Their home radiated peace. I might be picking me up some sage on the ride home.

Once Greta was done, she sat down next to us. "Okay. Which one of you is going first?"

Molly and I looked at each other. I reached behind me and picked up my box.

"Okay, what do I do?"

"Release him."

I sighed and clutched the small cardboard box tightly in my arms, trying to figure out what 'Release him' meant in terms of standing in front of a fire with a box full of stuff. I didn't have anything that actually belonged to George, so on Greta's instructions, I had purchased things that represented him. The first item I pulled out of the box was a Harley-Davidson T-shirt.

"George," I said. My voice was faltering. I felt like an idiot. And that fire was hot. I stepped back and turned to Greta. "I feel like an idiot."

Greta stood up. She took the T-shirt from me and smiled kindly at me. "Let me get you started."

She held up the T-shirt to the heavens. "George Lewis, this is Wanda, releasing you." She threw the shirt into the fire. The blaze grew a bit, then died down. She turned to me.

"What's next?"

I reached in the box and pulled out a girlie magazine.

"George, this is me, releasing you." I threw it in the fire. Naked woman after naked woman curled up and burned.

It felt good. I threw more items in the fire, gaining more enthusiasm for the process as I went. Next was a bumper sticker that read "Don't like my driving? Call 1-800-EATSHIT," followed by chewing tobacco. In hindsight, I probably should have taken it out of the plastic case first. When the black smoke cleared, I threw in a dangling skull-and-crossbones earring, which wouldn't really burn, but it was more about the gesture, anyway. As each item went into the fire, I released him. It felt good. It felt right. Even if I woke up the next day feeling just as crappy as I had that morning, at least for a brief shining moment, I felt as though it was me being released.

Greta was definitely onto something.

Finally, all that remained in the box was the St. Erasmus medal and a bottle of Jim Beam.

I handed the bottle to Molly and winked at her. "This is George's gift to us."

She smiled. I walked over to Greta and gave her the medal.

"I want to keep this. Can you do your sage thing with it? You know, smudge all the negative energy away?"

She grabbed the smoking hunk of weeds from the edge of the fire.

An hour later, after Molly had released her ex into the flames, we were all sitting on the logs, watching the fire wane, drinking Jim Beam and Coke from plastic cups. We talked about our histories. I found out that Molly had lesbian tendencies before George ever touched her. Greta was an artist and made jewelry that she sold at local shows. Molly was freelancing as a marketing consultant. They agreed to come down to Hastings and get their pictures taken with Santa Bones.

"Trust me," I said. "It will be the best day of Bones's life."

Later, curled up in a tent with two lesbians and one tremendous dog, I fell into one of the deepest, most comfortable sleeps I'd had in a long, long time.

And when I woke up, I still felt good.

My mind was racing through the entire ride home. It was a good thing I had St. Erasmus around my neck, helping me navigate, because when I pulled into Elizabeth's driveway, I couldn't remember driving back.

I opened the front door. Elizabeth was on the sofa, reading. Kacey was sitting on the living room floor, the PlayStation wide open and guts hanging all over the place. I dropped my bag on the floor.

Elizabeth dropped her book and hopped up off the sofa.

"Thanks for calling, doofus! I was so worried about you." She ran over and hugged me, then gave me a semiplayful push. "You scared the hell out of me. What were you thinking? I was this close to calling the police!"

I cringed. "Oh, man. I'm sorry. I didn't think about it."

Elizabeth gave me a light smack on the back of the head. "Call next time! People worry."

I smiled at her, trying to come up with something to say. I'd been alone for so long that it hadn't even occurred to me that anyone would be worried by my taking off for a day. She turned and headed toward the kitchen. "I have to call Walter. I called him to see if you stayed at his place last night. He's been out looking for you ever since."

"Oh, Christ," I said, rubbing my hand over my forehead, feeling like a big dope.

"Unless . . . ," she said, pausing and jerking her head gently in the direction of the phone. "Do you want to call him?"

Yes. I shook my head. "Tell him I'm sorry."

She nodded and retreated into the kitchen to make the call. I took a few tentative steps toward Kacey.

"Hey, Kace. PlayStation broken again?"

Kacey didn't even look up. I could tell from her stiff movements that she was upset. I walked over and sat down next to her, being careful not to step on any random parts. I gave her shoulder a gentle shove with mine.

"Kace, I'm sorry. Really. I wasn't thinking. I had some stuff I needed to deal with."

She turned her face toward me a little. "We didn't know where you were."

"I know," I said, feeling like a teen who'd been out past curfew.

"You could have been dead on the side of the road."

"I know. I know. I'm sorry."

She pushed her glasses up on her nose and examined my face for signs of true regret. I must have passed the test, because a moment later she threw her arms around my neck and hugged me tight. I put my arms around her little body and squeezed. She released me and gave me a sharp pinch on my arm for good measure, then smiled.

"Alex is in his room. He's been pretending not to be worried, but you should go tell him you're here."

I ruffled her hair and headed up the stairs. The door to Alex's room stood closed like an ominous barrier at the end of the hall. I'd never been in the inner sanctum before. I rapped twice on the door.

"Alex? It's me."

I heard some shuffling, then, "Come in."

I opened the door. He was sitting cross-legged at the head of his bed, his back slumped against a husband pillow. There were a few crumpled pages on the floor, and a pen was resting by his foot. The edge of the leather journal I'd bought him hung out of a hastily shut drawer in his desk. I smiled.

"Just wanted you to know I was home safe."

He shrugged. "I knew you would be. The girls were all freaking out."

Ah. *The girls.* I withheld my smile and sat down on the corner of his bed and glanced toward the desk.

"So . . . you been writing in that journal?"

His eyes widened a bit. Busted. He regained his cool and shrugged again. "A little."

I nodded. "Anything good?"

He shrugged. " 'Sokay."

"Would you let me read it?"

His posture straightened a bit, but that was all I got, aside from a barely perceptible nod. We sat for a second in silence. I stood up. "Well, I'm sorry if I worried you."

"I wasn't worried."

I was at the door when I heard my name. I turned around. He was holding the journal out to me. "I wrote a play for your stupid puppet show."

I raised my eyebrows. "Is it good?"

He shrugged. "Kids might like it."

I took the journal and grinned at him. "Think you can help me get a performance together by Christmas Eve?"

He shrugged again. I sat back down on the bed.

"Look, Alex, let me tell you something so you don't end up wasting a bunch of precious time. If there's something you care about, just own up to it and go for it. If you get hit by a bus tomorrow, do you want to die knowing the only thing you ever did was pretend you didn't care about anything?"

His eyes widened. "You're getting preachy in your old age."

I smiled. "There. An actual statement of opinion. We're getting somewhere. Now, back to my original question: do you give enough of a shit about what you wrote to help me put a show on?"

He smiled. "You said 'shit.'"

I held up the journal. "I'll read it tonight. Meantime, I want you at the Santa Station every day after school, okay? I'll clear it with your mom."

"Okay," he said. I squeezed his foot and stood up, almost out of the room before he called my name again.

"What?" I said, turning around.

"I'm glad you're home," he said.

I smiled. "Me, too, kid."

❧

I closed the journal after reading Alex's play and stared at the ceiling in my apartment. The kid was a writer. There were some rough spots—he had a couple of grammatical issues—but he was a writer. His story was funny, his characters were sharp, and his dialogue wasn't half-bad.

He was a writer.

I gave a short chuckle, staring down at the journal clutched in my hand.

"Hmph," I said to no one. "Who knew?"

I leaned over on my side and looked at my wall. Just five stickies left.

Go see parents.

Do something meaningful.

Identify phantom music.

Figure out what I want.

Tell Walter.

I flipped through Alex's journal, looking at the chicken scratch. I reached over, pulled *Do something meaningful* off the wall, and threw it into the garbage can. Cuddling Alex's journal to my chin, I fell asleep, smiling.

12

I'd been lying on my bed for an hour since getting home. As Christmas approached, things at the Santa Station had been getting out of hand. I'd been dragging that damn train full of kids all day. My back hurt. My legs throbbed. My eyelashes were tired.

And I was still hearing that damn phantom music.

There was a small knock at the door. I didn't move.

"Come in!"

Kacey opened the door, her arms loaded with a tray carrying two glasses of milk and a plate of what smelled like fresh-baked chocolate chip cookies. I sat up.

"You are the best kid on the planet," I said, getting up to help her with the tray. We settled on opposite ends of my bed, digging into the cookies and milk, addressing priorities before we bothered with small talk. It wasn't until Kacey was well into her second cookie that I heard her humming.

My tune.

"Kace?" I said. "Why are you humming that?"

"Hmmm?" She looked up at me, the tiniest trace of a milk mustache on her lips. I smiled.

"The song. My song. You were humming it. Have you heard it recently?"

She sighed. "No. That's the problem."

"What do you mean?"

She leaned forward, tossing up her hands in exaggerated preteen frustration. "Wanda, I've listened to everything. Wagner. Berlioz. Tchaikovsky. I've been to the library. I've borrowed stuff from my friends' parents. Brittany's grandfather plays in the symphony, and I hummed it for him and he didn't know it. I couldn't find it. I'm sorry."

I opened my mouth, came up with nothing, closed it again. I stared down at the crumbs swimming on the surface of my milk. I could feel my eyes filling with tears as I looked back up at her angelic little face. "Thanks, kid."

Her eyes widened. "What's the matter with you?"

I shrugged and tried to catch my breath as the tears came faster. "Nothing . . . just . . . you . . . that you would do that . . . for me . . ." I threw my hands up in the air and went into the bathroom to grab a roll of toilet paper, blowing my nose and tossing the crumpled mass into the garbage can, then sat on the bed again.

Kacey laughed. "You're weird. Why wouldn't I do that for you? You're family."

"Stop!" I said, fresh tears sprouting. "What are you trying to do, kill me?"

She shook her head. "Grown-ups cry over the strangest things, don't they?"

I laughed and nodded. "Yeah. Sometimes." I looked up at her and managed a quivering smile. "Really. Don't be freaked out. I'm fine. It's just . . ." I waved my hand in front of my face, trying to fan the emotion away. "I love you, kid."

She laughed and hopped over to my side of the bed, throwing her arms around my neck. "I love you, too, Wanda."

As I wrapped my arms around her, I got my first glimpse of the unconditional love parents feel for their children. It was a quick snapshot, an intense burst of emotion that radiated through me, and I knew that I would step in front of a train for her without thinking twice. I would kill anyone who ever tried to hurt her. And if she ever strapped herself to the back of some loser's Harley, I would never stop loving her, no matter how many stupid mistakes she made.

I gave her a quick squeeze and grabbed the roll of toilet paper again, wiping my eyes and trying to put on a brave face for her.

"They're happy tears," I said.

"Yeah," she said as she stood up. "I think you'll be okay."

"You know what, kid?" I said, putting my arm around her as I walked her to the door. "I think so, too."

I sent her back downstairs and sat on my bed, staring at the four stubborn stickies left on my wall. I pulled down *Go see parents*, staring at the letters on the paper, wondering at how a bunch of marker squiggles on some processed pulp could hold so much power. I stuck it back on the wall with the others and called the airlines to get rates for a trip to New York City for Saturday morning.

☙☙

I hate flying. It doesn't make sense that a multi-ton piece of machinery carrying hundreds of people can stay in the air just because it's moving really fast. I realize that millions of flights zoom all over the country without event every year and that flying is statistically safer than driving, but I still found myself digging my fingernails into the armrests while staring out the window, as though the plane would drop out of the sky if I didn't keep my eyes attached to the clouds.

We landed safely in New York, just as the stewardess predicted. I didn't find out until after I'd referred to her as a stewardess that they were called flight attendants now. I spent much of the flight trying to think of a clever, irritatingly PC nickname for "passenger," until I realized that it didn't do much to divert my attention from the real source of my anxiety, and so I turned to crossword puzzles.

My return flight was open-ended. I could leave that night, or I could leave in the morning. Elizabeth and Bones and the kids had assured me the Santa Station could live without me for a day. Now the only thing left to worry about was whether I was about to experience a happy reunion or flat parental rejection.

On with the show.

It wasn't until I was halfway to Chappaqua in my rental car that I reconsidered my decision not to call first. It was

December 23. They could be anywhere. Dad had retired from the firm in the city some years back and started a small practice in town, but he never worked Christmas week anymore. Maybe they'd be spending the day with Aunt Margaret in Hoboken. Maybe they would take a few days and do Christmas in the city. Maybe Mom wouldn't be home cooking dinner. Maybe they were out nabbing some Chinese and a movie.

Maybe the whole trip would be a bust and I'd have to come back and my whole plan would fall apart and . . .

My train of thought stopped short as I pulled into the driveway.

They were home.

Through the huge living room window, I could see Dad sitting in his chair, reading the paper. Mom came out, refilled his glass of wine, and leaned in for the quick thank-you kiss that'd been part of their routine since I could remember.

Suddenly, my heart ached for routine.

I hoisted my bag over my shoulder and forced my legs to carry me up the driveway to the front door. I never knew ankles could shake, but mine seemed about ready to give up and drop me.

I hit the doorbell and briefly considered running, until I saw my father glance through the living room window to see who was there, disappear, and then come back, his face registering recognition this time.

Must have been the hair. I was sure he couldn't recall having given life to a giant match. I ran my hands over my head, and there was my father standing before me, door open. Tall.

Gray. Silent. I reached into my bag and pulled out a bottle of Chivas Regal, holding it out to him.

"I brought you something," I said, trying to breathe.

He reached out and took it from me, staring down at it for a moment before looking back up at me.

"Thank you," he said, and smiled.

That's what did it. The smile. It's shocking how powerful a smile from your father can be. I stood where I was and felt the tears fall down my face. *Goof,* I thought. *Doofus. Say what you came here to say.*

"I'm sorry," I said, barely a whisper. I looked up and caught his face and he was crying, too, and he pulled me into his arms and kissed me on the top of my head, the way he used to do after my recitals at Miss Maria's School of Dance.

"There's nothing to be sorry for, honey," he said quietly into my hair.

"Jonathan?" I heard my mother's wary tones come up over Dad's shoulder. He released me, swiped his hand over his face, and turned slightly, clearing the way between my mother and me.

Her eyes fixed on me and paused. Eight years and a wacky haircut were hell on recognition. When the moment hit, her eyebrows knit together briefly, and she looked at my father. He nodded at her, and she froze, her hands still clutched to her apron in a gesture of perpetual drying.

I reached into my bag and pulled out the first English edition of *Anna Karenina* that Bones had let me have at a hell of a discount and handed it to her.

"I brought you something," I said, my voice crackling as I spoke.

She released her apron and took the book from me, running her hands lightly across the cover. I tried to concentrate on breathing, steadied myself, and then looked at her. When her eyes rose from the book to me, I spoke again.

"I understand now," I said, falling back on memorization and rehearsal to get through it. "I didn't for a long time, but now I do. George is gone. Long gone. I'm living in Tennessee, and I have a life there. I like it. But I wanted to come here and tell you how sorry I am."

My mother calmly put the book on the small table by the door and stepped forward, putting her arms around my neck and pulling me in for a hug.

"We love you, honey," she said. "I hope you always knew that."

"I knew," I said, although I hadn't, not really, not until I heard the words.

Dad stepped back and ushered me into the house, and we settled into the living room. Mom went to fill some glasses with ice, and Dad went to work opening the Chivas.

"Have you developed a taste for Scotch?" he asked. "I remember you hating the stuff when you were younger."

"I've changed a little," I said.

He looked at me and grinned. "I can see that. I like the hair."

Mom came in with the glasses, and Dad filled them, and the whole scene was surreal in its serene domesticity. She handed me a glass and sat down next to me on the sofa. Her eyes were red, and it looked like she'd been crying in the kitchen, but Dad and I didn't say anything. Either one of us could crack at any moment, so there was nothing to be gained in pointing fingers.

"So how have you been?" she asked quietly.

"Good," I said. "I'm divorced. Single. Living over a friend's garage."

I saw my parents exchange glances, and I berated myself for testing them. Old habits die hard. I smiled.

"I own my own business. I've been seeing a lawyer."

My father's face brightened. "Really?"

"Yeah," I said, not worrying that Walter and I weren't technically dating at the moment. I was taking it one sticky note at a time. "He reminds me of you a bit, Dad."

Dad smiled. "Sounds like a good man."

"Yeah," I said, taking another sip of my drink and feeling a small smile emerge on my lips. "He really is."

∽

It was the middle of the night. I woke up in my old room, which hadn't changed since the day I left. I sat up in bed, staring at the faded, curling eighties heartthrob posters on the wall, hearing phantom strands of that goddamn song.

Again.

I'd been hoping that it had something to do with this visit. That it would just go away, magically, as soon as I resolved things with my parents. Apparently, I'd been engaging in what the kids today call wishful thinking.

I threw my feet over the side and slid them into my old slippers. I laughed. I couldn't believe they still had my stupid slippers.

I saw light from the television flickering over the living room as I came down the stairs. Dad was sitting on the couch, futzing with the remote while *The Philadelphia Story* played silently in the background. I smiled.

"Hey," I said.

He looked up, his face chagrined. "I'm sorry. I couldn't sleep, so I put the tape in. It started out pretty loud . . ."

I waved him off. "I was awake." I jerked my chin toward the television. "Haven't seen that in a while."

He grinned. "Me neither."

"How about you rewind it and turn the sound back on, and I'll go get us some ice cream?"

He nodded. "Sounds perfect. Thanks."

I padded into the kitchen and stuck my head into the freezer. There were three pints of Ben & Jerry's Cherry Garcia.

"You're a good man, Mom," I said, grabbing one pint and two spoons and heading back into the living room.

I froze. There it was. The music. The phantom music I'd been hearing all along.

The theme from *The Philadelphia Story*.

"Oh my God," I said. Dad turned around and looked at me.

"Wanda?" he said, concern thick in his voice. "Are you okay?"

I nodded, swiping at my face with the back of one hand and coming around the sofa to sit next to him. I pulled the top off the ice cream and handed him a spoon.

"When did we start doing this, Dad?" I asked, trying to keep my voice even. "Watching *The Philadelphia Story* every Christmas?"

He shrugged, taking a dig from the ice cream. "I don't know. We had it on tape when you were a kid."

I nodded. From the corner of my eye, I could see him watching me.

"Wanda?" he said. "Are you sure you're okay?"

I looked up at him and smiled, snuggling next to him. He put his arm around my shoulders and pulled me close. I felt twelve again. Safe. Loved.

At home.

And I knew at that moment exactly what I wanted and whom I wanted it with.

"That theme music," I said. "That's not even close to a classical style, is it?"

He laughed. "Not really, no."

I licked my spoon and laughed. Dad sighed.

"It's good to have you back, Wanda. I wish you would stay for Christmas."

"I can't," I said. "I have plans tomorrow night. But . . ." I sat up and looked at him. "Mom's birthday is in February. Why don't you guys come out for a visit? I'd love for you to meet my friends."

"And your young man," he said, raising an eyebrow.

I smiled and snuggled back next to him and settled in for two glorious hours of Katharine Hepburn and Cary Grant.

And Jimmy Stewart.

"Anne Marie keeps forgetting her line right before the spaceship comes down," Alex said, wringing his hands as he sat down next to me. It was Christmas Eve, and Osgiliath's was packed full. The Santa Station was doing triple its regular business, and the seats we'd set up in front of the puppet show were starting to fill. T minus thirty minutes, and Alex was beginning to unravel.

"Don't worry about it," I said, clicking the remote control on the camera and typing the name of the little boy on Bones's knee into the NASCAR-themed border I'd chosen for him. "I gave her an Itty Bitty Book Light and a copy of the script. It'll be fine."

"Do you think it's too weird?" he said. "You know, having Santa Claus be an alien?"

I laughed. "I think it's great. It's a great play, you're doing a great job. Now, relax." The printer whined as Anne Marie pulled another kid out of the train and ushered him to Bones.

"What if they all laugh?" he asked. "What if they *don't* laugh?"

I put my arm around his shoulders. "If you were twenty-one, I'd make you take a drink. As it is, I need that camera shot lined up. Go to work, boy."

I picked up the printout and placed it inside the cardboard frame, standing up to give it to the father of the little boy in it. I looked up with a smile into a nasty little pencil face.

"Oh, man," I said under my breath. Pencil Face was gripping his child's hand so tightly I thought the poor kid was going to start crying. He was a pudgy kid, looked to be about nine or ten, wearing a brown suit and loafers, and in his eyes I saw the fearful reflections of a thousand playground bullies.

"Exactly what is this?" Pencil Face hissed.

"It's a picture." I handed it to the boy and gave him a wink, which was met with a small smile that never reached his eyes. I stood up and crossed my arms, looking for any sign of recognition from Pencil Face. There was none. I was just another bug to wipe off the windshield when he was done, same as before.

The kid opened up the folded cardboard with his free hand. "Cool. NASCAR."

Pencil Face gave his kid's arm a jerk for good measure. I glared at him. "What exactly is your problem, sir?"

"Santa Claus," he spat, jerking his head toward Bones, "is *black*."

"Oh, for crying out loud," I said. "Are you kidding me?"

"What am I supposed to tell my kid," he said, "when he comes here and sees a black fucking Santa Claus?"

"Whatever you say," I hissed back, "you should watch your language."

His eyes narrowed into slits. "I want my money back. I didn't pay eight bucks for my kid to be sitting on the lap of a black damn Santa Claus."

I rolled my eyes and went into the cash box, grabbing eight dollars and thrusting it back at him, and wishing I'd knocked his lights out when I had the chance. The boy, with an expression of disappointment if not surprise, held the picture out to me. I leaned down and gently put it back in his hands. "You keep that, kid. Merry Christmas."

The kid smiled up at me, then looked tentatively to Pencil Face.

Pencil Face rolled his eyes at the kid and spat, "Fine. Keep it," as he dragged the kid away. I watched them leave, wishing I could grab that kid and hug away the crap that came with having Pencil Face for a father. Unfortunately, there was no fixing some things.

"It's time," Alex said, coming up behind me and tugging on my shirtsleeve. I turned and saw the excited face of a virgin playwright and put my arm around his shoulders.

"Let's go."

There were enough seats for thirty people, but Alex and I were left standing in the back with about twenty other late-comers as *Santa Claus Is from Salkog-9* began. Jack, Kacey, Elizabeth, and Matt found their way through the crowd, and we all surrounded Alex as the show got under way.

I glanced at Alex a few times during the show. His eyes were locked intently on the puppets, his lips moving with the lines as they were said. He smiled when lines got laughs, and frowned during a couple of unintended twitters. I'd never seen the kid so involved in anything. At the end, when everyone did a standing ovation, the players came out for their bows, waving for Alex to join them. As he took his bows with the troupe, Elizabeth nudged me with her shoulder, and we laughed as we realized we were both crying. Kacey looked up at us and rolled her eyes. *Grown-ups.*

At the party afterward, I sidled up to Jack and put my arm through his as we watched Elizabeth proudly showing Alex off, with Matt at her side.

"How ya doin'?" I asked.

He looked down at me and smiled. "I'm fine."

"If it means anything," I said, motioning my cup of punch toward Matt, "he's a bit of a Ken doll."

Jack laughed, taking a sip of his punch. "Yeah, but he makes her happy, doesn't he?"

I nodded. "Yeah. He does."

He tossed his empty cup in a nearby trash can and gave me a quick hug. "I gotta go. Can you tell Elizabeth I'll be by to get the kids around two tomorrow?"

I smiled. "Sure."

"Thanks," he said. "You gonna be there?"

"No," I said. "I've got plans."

"Okay, well, merry Christmas." He hugged me again, then slipped out quietly. I watched him go. No matter how cool Matt was, and no matter how rotten Jack had been, I knew I'd always hold a torch for Jack and Elizabeth. But what's none of my business is none of my business, and I had my own screwed-up life to attend to.

I felt an arm link through mine and was practically knocked over by Shelley's mammoth stomach.

"That kid homesteading or what?" I asked. "Aren't you due yet?"

She shook her head, taking a sip of punch. "No. I'm not due until January fifth."

I could see her belly button protruding through her shirt.

"That's it," I said. "I'm definitely adopting little girls from China."

She smiled. "I'm glad you'll be here with Bones. It makes me feel better about leaving."

I shrugged. "It's only six weeks. Or was it eight weeks? When are you coming back again?"

She knit her eyebrows at me. "Did Bones tell you I was coming back?"

I sucked in some breath. "You're not coming back?"

She shook her head and laughed. "That old sneak. He told me you'd agreed to take the position permanently."

I laughed and looked over at Bones entertaining the kids with an animated reading of "The Night Before Christmas."

"So," she said, "will you stay?"

I patted her arm. "Are you kidding? How could I pass up the chance to bug Bones on a full-time basis?"

She squeezed my hand. "I'm glad. I'll get with you next week and we'll go over the details." She started to walk away, then turned around. "Make sure he pays you well."

I grinned. "I will."

I watched Shelley waddle over to stand near Bones. Matt and Elizabeth were fawning over Alex by the refreshments. Kacey was standing on her own nearby. I caught her eye and waved her over.

"Geez," she said. "You'd think he'd just opened on Broadway, the way Mom's gushing over him."

"I'm proud of your brother," I said, "and I'd lecture you on the fact that you should be, too, but we've got work to do. You ready?"

She flashed her grin at me. "I'm always ready."

Osgiliath's was dark, with the exception of the fire-hazard–worthy crop of tiny white Christmas lights Kacey and I had strung all over the Santa Station. I paced back and forth in front of my desk, trying to kill time. I checked the clock on the computer: 11:48.

Twelve minutes.

I'd put the finishing touches on a half hour ago, and sitting still was only making time slow down. I got up and wandered over to the artificial Christmas tree we'd put up in the corner behind the Santa throne. Underneath were all the fake gifts, with the exception of one that I'd placed there two hours before. I walked by the long plate-glass windows on the west side of the store, checking out my reflection in the mirror. Elizabeth had loaned me her long, green, clingy holiday dress, and I had to admit I looked good. I patted my hair and checked my makeup, which Elizabeth had talked me into at the last minute and which I was beginning to regret. I hate lipstick. But what's done is done, and it was too late now.

I wandered back to the brightly lit Station and checked the camera and the software. Made sure the printer was full with the fancy glossy stuff. I wandered over to Santa's throne, fiddled with some of the lights, and finally plopped down in the seat. I looked at my watch: 11:56.

Four minutes.

I leaned back in the Santa throne, staring up at the ceiling. I smiled when I heard the familiar jingle at the front door, which I'd left unlocked. A moment later, Walter appeared from behind a bookshelf.

He was dressed in a tailored tan suit with a dark green tie. I sucked in my breath. He took off his coat and placed it on the swivel seat by the computer, but he never moved his eyes from mine. I stood up and smoothed out my dress.

"You look beautiful," he said, walking toward me.

"I'm glad you showed up. I was afraid you might not know who sent the note."

He laughed. "A mysterious note on my doorstep tells me to be at Osgiliath's at midnight. I took a shot in the dark." He stopped about three feet away from me and put his hands in his trouser pockets. His smile was soft and assured. "I'm glad I was right."

I stood up and walked over to meet him. He reached out for my waist, and I put my hand to his chest, pushing him back lightly. "Not yet, cowboy. We need to talk."

I grabbed his hand and led him toward the velvet-lined platform that housed the Santa throne.

His fingers tightened, entwining with mine. "You're right. We do need to talk. I haven't forgotten that you scared the hell out of me when you took off like that."

"Yeah, I wasn't planning on talking about that now. Can I just apologize and breeze on past that?"

"That all depends on what you've got planned," he said, his eyes running around the Station and then landing back on me. "If you distract me well enough, I might be able to let it go." His eyes took on a devilish glint. "But I'm not that easily distracted."

I smiled and put my hands on his shoulders. He reached for

my waist. I gently pushed him down into the Santa throne. I sat on the platform at his feet and flashed my hands over the dress, smoothing it around my legs, then looked up at Walter. Lit by the tiny white Christmas lights, he looked more like Jimmy Stewart than ever. Indescribable elegance wrapped in undeniable masculinity.

He looked down at me, and I realized I'd been staring at him for a while and saying nothing. "Did you have something to say?"

"Yes," I said, nerves gripping my heart in an icy vise. I felt perspiration forming on the back of my neck. I'd practiced my whole speech a hundred times, and now I was choking. I stood up and began to pace.

Walter started to get up. "Are you okay?"

I put my hand out. "No, sit, please. I'm trying to do this right, but . . . Oh, hell. It's not going to be right." I turned to face him. "Walter, I love you."

Oh, man. Going to throw up. Going to throw up all over Elizabeth's nice dress. I put my hand on my stomach and continued to pace. "I'm sorry. I wanted this to be so romantic. I don't know what I'm doing. I've never done this before, loved someone who was actually capable of loving me back . . . Not that you have to, and please don't say if you do or not, because I can't hear it right now either way . . ."

I was wringing my hands so tight the skin was starting to burn. I turned to face him, glanced at him for a brief moment, then snapped my eyes shut and continued to babble. "Not long after . . . that night when . . . you know, we did it . . ." *Oh, man. Did it? What am I, nineteen?* ". . . I kinda freaked out."

He smiled. "Yeah. I figured as much. I wish you had just called me . . ."

I held up my hand. "Ah-ah-ah. Not done. I'm sorry, I just need to get through this, and if you talk, I'm going to melt all over you."

He broke out his crooked grin and raised an eyebrow at me. "I don't have a problem with that."

"Ahhhhh," I said. "You're killing me. Work with me here."

He sat back and closed his lips in a smile. I continued to pace in front of him, closing my eyes as I spoke, trying to remember how I'd planned this. "Where was I? Oh, yeah. Freaked out. So I sat down with myself and tried to figure out what was wrong with me. Why I had certain patterns in my life that were so self-destructive, and I realized . . . well . . ."

I opened my eyes. He was smiling. *Kryptonite.* I sat down on the platform at his feet. "It was a self-fulfilling prophecy, you know? People were always telling me how smart I was, how I was destined for great things, and I always thought, someday they'll find out. They'll find out I'm a fraud, and I'm worthless, and I'm . . ."

I was starting to choke up. I stood up again and paced. "It was stupid. I wasn't making bad choices because I was worthless, I was making bad choices to show I was worthless, so I wouldn't have to ever stand up and . . . I don't know. Fall, I guess. But I did worse than fall. I deliberately fucked it all up, so very, very badly."

I looked at him briefly, until my throat started to close, and looked away again. "In order to unravel all the crap I'd gotten myself into, I decided I'd have to do certain things . . . to make it up to myself. To clean the slate, you know? So I made up this list, and I thought if I followed it, changed who I was, then I'd be worthy of you."

I stopped and stared at the floor. Walter was blurred through my tears, and a distant voice in the back of my head warned of raccoon eyes, but I kept going. "I did it all. Everything."

I took a deep breath and wiped under my eyes. Black on my fingers. Stupid mascara. I went to the computer and grabbed a Kleenex and walked back toward Walter, still not looking at him. "And now that I'm all done, I finally understand."

I stopped. Walter stood up. He put his hand on my arm and spoke quietly. "Understand what?"

"That it was all a load of crap," I squeaked. God, I had no idea how hard this would be to say. "I was perfectly worthy of you to begin with, and if you didn't see that, then you were a big, stupid doofus."

His eyebrows knit, and he let out a small laugh and shook his head.

"Well, duh." He put his forehead to mine and pulled my hands to his chest. "How could you not know that?"

"I don't know," I said. My voice was quivering, as were my lips, my entire body. I rested my forehead against his and got my balance. "But that's why I called you here tonight. I thought I'd give you a second chance."

He chuckled. "I'm glad you did."

I looked up at him, and he smiled down at me, his eyes glittering in the reflection of a thousand Christmas lights. He leaned down and brushed his lips lightly against mine.

"I'm going to explode if you don't say it's okay for me to kiss you soon," he whispered, his cool breath fluttering into my mouth.

Unable to speak, I nodded and felt his hand come up around the back of my neck as he pressed his lips on mine, and we melted into each other, kisses coming in perfect rhythm with the boom-boom-booming of my heart.

We parted and stood there for a while, dancing slowly to the silence. He ran his hand over my hair, down my back, and rested it on my waist. I draped my arms around his shoulders and leaned my cheek against his chest and felt safe. Loved.

At home.

"I meant it," he said softly.

"Hmmm?"

"That night," he said, pulling me in tighter and resting his cheek on the top of my head. "When I said I loved you."

I pulled away. "You remember that?"

"Hell, yeah, I remember," he said, smoothing a stray strand of hair away from my face. "I've been beating myself up over it every day since. It was a stupid thing to say, but I was falling asleep and I just wasn't thinking."

"How could you have meant that?" I asked. "You barely even knew me."

He shook his head, a mystified smile on his lips. "I don't know. I guess I knew enough. But it was too early. I don't blame you for running off."

I grinned. "Could you tell me again?"

"What? That I love you?"

I nodded. He put both hands on either side of my face and looked into my eyes. "God help me, but I love you, Wanda Lane."

I smiled. "I like it. Lose the 'God help me' next time, though, okay?"

He gave me a quick kiss on the forehead. "Deal."

I stepped away and grabbed his hand. "We're not done yet."

He laughed and pulled me back to him. "I was hoping not."

I scrambled from his grip and led him to the Santa throne, sitting him down again. "Stay right here."

I set up the shot in the camera, grabbed the remote, and rushed over to him, sitting on his lap. I held his face in my hands and clicked the remote, which was followed by a flash from the camera.

"Shouldn't we be looking at the camera?" he asked, not taking his eyes off mine.

"Oh, we're not done," I said, tossing the remote aside. "I set it up for ten pictures."

He kissed me. The flash went off. We smiled for the camera, and it flashed. The flashes went on around us, capturing the moment as we posed and giggled like teenagers.

After a while, I led him back to the Christmas tree and handed him a carefully wrapped box. He sighed. "I'm sorry, Wanda, I didn't think to bring your present . . ."

I shushed him and walked over to the computer, leaning

over it and looking at our shots. He walked up behind me and put his hand on the small of my back. It fit perfectly.

We pored over the shots together, arguing playfully until we chose a favorite. It was one where we were sitting, smiling into each other's eyes. I clicked print and turned to him, motioning toward the present.

"Open it."

He sighed and opened the package, pulling out a simple wooden picture frame. I grabbed the picture from the printer and handed it to him.

"I think it's time you started putting some new pictures on your mantel."

Quietly, he put the picture in the frame and turned it over, running his fingers lightly across the figures under the glass. I didn't notice the stray tear on his cheek until he turned to me and smiled.

"Thank you." He pulled me into his arms. "I love it."

I snuggled my cheek next to his chest, listening to the boom-boom-booming of his heart, inhaling his scent. It was good. It was all good.

"Hmmm," I heard him hum above me. "How are you feeling?"

I raised my head and smiled into his eyes.

"Never better," I said. And damned if that wasn't the truth.

About the Author

Lani Diane Rich's first job was at the age of eleven, when she combined her love of books with an overdeveloped sense of ambition and volunteered at her local library. She has been writing stories and screenplays since she could pick up a pen, but never pursued writing because—well, really, who ever makes it as an author? She graduated from Syracuse University's Newhouse School in 1998 with a degree in television production, and has been, in no particular order, a pyrotechnician, a nanny, a convenience store clerk, a theater critic, and an associate producer of an Alaska newsmagazine. She wrote the original draft of her first novel, *Time Off for Good Behavior*, in twenty-five days while participating in National Novel Writing Month 2002 (www.nanowrimo.org), and decided on December 31 of that year to dedicate 2003 to seriously pursuing her writing. Now she works in her pajamas, and she really, really likes it.